Blaze

Dear Reader,

Wouldn't it be nice if everything were either black or white? Good or evil? Wrong or right? Honestly, though, don't you think it would also be unbearably boring? It's one of the reasons we take great thrill in exploring the shades of gray that come between.

In *Unbridled*, hot, suspended Marine Carter Southard (from *Branded*) is cleared by sexy defense attorney Laney Cartwright of a civilian crime he didn't commit, but he still must jump through military hoops if he hopes to be reinstated. As out of his league as Laney may be, he can't help wanting to mess up her pristine existence just a little bit. But when steamy, no-strings sex evolves into much, much more, they must wrestle with their preconceptions of each other... as well as their own misconceptions of themselves.

We hope you enjoy Carter and Laney's sizzling and sometimes heart-wrenching journey toward sexily-ever-after. We'd love to hear what you think. Contact us at P.O. Box 12271, Toledo, OH 43612 (we'll respond with a signed bookplate, newsletter and bookmark), or visit us on the Web at www.toricarrington.net.

Here's wishing you love, romance and *hot* reading.

Lori and Tony Karayianni
aka Tori Carrington

Tori Carrington

UNBRIDLED

HOURLY CHECK

Date __6-9-09__ Time __20:00__

Act-up __1__ Ties __1__

Quality __2__ Appearance __2__

Glue
Application __1__ Dip __1__

Superviser __P9__

HARLEQUIN®

TORONTO • NEW YORK • LONDON
AMSTERDAM • PARIS • SYDNEY • HAMBURG
STOCKHOLM • ATHENS • TOKYO • MILAN • MADRID
PRAGUE • WARSAW • BUDAPEST • AUCKLAND

ISBN-13: 978-0-373-79487-4

UNBRIDLED

Copyright © 2009 by Lori and Tony Karayianni.

ABOUT THE AUTHOR

Romantic Times BOOKreviews Career Achievement Award-winning, bestselling husband-and-wife duo Lori and Tony Karayianni are the power behind the pen name Tori Carrington. Their forty novels include numerous Harlequin Blaze miniseries, as well as the ongoing Sofie Metropolis, PI, comedic mystery series with another publisher. Visit www.toricarrington.net and www.sofiemetro.com for more information on the couple and their titles.

Books by Tori Carrington

Don't miss any of our special offers. Write to us at the following address for information on our newest releases.

Harlequin Reader Service
U.S.: 3010 Walden Ave., P.O. Box 1325, Buffalo, NY 14269
Canadian: P.O. Box 609, Fort Erie, Ont. L2A 5X3

We dedicate this book to fellow shades-of-gray travelers everywhere: enjoy the journey! And, as always, to our editor extraordinaire Brenda Chin, who has a knack for seeing the forest and the trees.

Prologue

FREEDOM WAS JUST a word…until you lost it. After you were put into a steel box and stripped of your personal belongings and your name, owning nothing more than a number and the crime for which you were charged.

"Inmate 55687, collect your things. You've been given your wings."

Carter Southard stared at the guard from where he lay on the hard top bunk in the four-by-nine-foot cell in the San Antonio County Jail. The words couldn't be meant for anyone else, because his bunk mate had been moved to a different cell the day before. Still, he couldn't help considering the imagery. He'd just been given his wings.

He closed the Steinbeck novel he was reading and got to his feet. He'd stopped even hoping for his release two days into his incarceration five days ago. Since he'd been wrongfully accused of a crime, there was no reason to believe things would be set right. Not so long as he was locked away, unable to prove his innocence.

And that had been the most difficult part. Not the injustice. Not that he'd been set up to pay for someone else's crime. But the loss of his freedom. Of his inability to fight back against an unseen enemy. Especially since his career in the Marines had always presented him with an identifiable target.

He gathered his few prison-issue toiletries and put them in the bag the guard provided and then stood Marine straight at the cell door. The guard motioned toward the block controller. The lock buzzed and the bars slid to the left. Carter turned so the guard could slap handcuffs on him and then turned around again.

Nearby inmates hooted and hollered as Carter followed the guard down the cell block. He kept his gaze forward, concentrating on the neat line of the other man's neck, urging him to speed up his steps. He wanted to get clear of the building before someone realized they'd made a mistake and locked him back in that damned cell.

What seemed like a lifetime later, a door was opened and the guard stepped aside, motioning Carter to precede him in. Carter was only too happy to oblige, keeping his eyes down.

Almost there…almost there…

The first thing he spotted was a pair of shiny beige high heels. Not the kind that strippers wore, but conservative, neat ones that had the height, but none of the zing.

The legs that belonged to the shoes, on the other hand, were nothing short of spectacular.

"Clear a path, inmate," the guard behind him ordered with a nudge of his nightstick.

Carter hadn't realized he'd stopped moving. He continued forward, the cuffs chafing his wrists behind his back. When he looked up, the woman was staring at him. And he felt as if the guard had just used that stick to whack him in the stomach.

He'd known women he'd trust at his side in a combat situation, something they were not legally permitted to do. But the woman in front of him was the complete opposite of any he'd find itching for a chance to fight on the front lines. She looked like a Kewpie doll, like the type of pinup girl men who had served in the Second World War might have taped inside their lockers. She had short, wavy blond hair, a perfectly oval face and flawless porcelain skin. Her bright blue eyes were wide, and her lips were shaped as if they were forever in pucker mode, waiting to be kissed.

Okay, it was official: he was losing it. He'd just spent the past five days swearing off all women. And he knew from experience that women like this one were exactly the kind to avoid at all costs. This bird would stick her bloodred talons straight into a man's chest and rip his heart out with arteries still fully attached.

The guard nudged him to turn and face him. He did, glad when the cuffs were removed. He absently rubbed his wrists and squinted at the woman, positive he was seeing things. Yes. Right now he was back in his cell, the Steinbeck novel in his hands, the woman before him a product of his imagination, an image sprung from the pages onto the blank wall of his unconscious mind.

Only not even his imagination was capable of conjuring the sweet smell of magnolias that engulfed him as she neared.

"Mr. Southard, I'm Laney Cartwright. Your attorney." She smiled. "I hope they treated you well."

His attorney? A couple of days ago he'd met with some snot-nosed public defender who'd looked as if he were two days out of grad school.

"I'm sorry—I've confused you," she said as the guard put the bag containing his belongings down on the counter next to the box of the clothes and watch and dog tags he'd been wearing, confiscated upon his arrest. "I've been hired by Trace Armstrong and a certain JoEllen Atchison to make sure you were released properly."

Carter stiffened at the mention of the couple responsible for his incarceration.

Miss June 1942 smiled again. "The real rapist has been caught. You're a free man, Mr. Southard."

Oh, yeah? If he was so free, why did he feel as if he'd gladly trade one prison cell for another so long as the leggy blonde was in it with him?

She looked at him a little too long. He tilted his head. She averted her gaze and then reached into her briefcase for something. She handed him what looked like the ring holding the key for his Harley.

"Mr. Armstrong arranged for your transportation to be delivered. It's outside now."

Carter raised his brows. If he didn't know better, Ms. Cartwright was as intrigued by him as he was by her. Which surprised him. While he'd come across his fair share of uptown women happy to slum it for a night or two, the attorney type barely looked twice at a man like him.

"Oh, here," she said, reaching into her briefcase again. "This is a letter of apology from Mr. Armstrong and Ms. Atchison. And while our business appears complete, should you need anything, this is my card with my office number in Dallas."

Dallas. Exactly where he was going.

Was it him, or did she put special emphasis on the word *anything?*

He grinned.

"As your attorney, it's my duty to strongly advise you to stay out of trouble, Mr. Southard."

She turned to walk away. Carter watched her go. He enjoyed the suggestive sway of her hips in the beige designer suit she wore, the long line of her legs and those naughty heels. He shook his head.

The last thing he needed in his life now was a woman. The most recent one had nearly proved to be the end of him.

"Way out of your league, Southard," the guard said, mirroring his own thoughts.

Carter slapped Ms. Cartwright's business card on the desk and swapped it for his personal effects. "Pass that on to someone who is in her league, won't you?"

And he turned toward the doors on his way to figure out the rest of his life. A life that would never include a woman like Laney Cartwright.

1

WHAT A DIFFERENCE two months made.

Or, rather, it was noteworthy how much the passage of time had affected Carter Southard's view of reality. He no longer woke up abruptly looking for a wall of bars that blocked him from the rest of the world. He didn't tense up when he passed a patrol officer on the road while driving his Harley, checking his rearview mirror to make sure the officer hadn't turned to follow him.

One thing that hadn't changed was the image of sexy Laney Cartwright standing in the jail's property room, handing him the freedom that had been ripped from him through no fault of his own. Her face was what he saw the moment he opened his eyes in the morning, and the last thing he thought about when he nodded off at night. And he wasn't granted a reprieve even then because his subconscious was given free rein over his unsatisfied desires and tortured him with fantasies involving the straitlaced defense attorney, fueling even more erotic images.

He hadn't seen her since then. But at least five times a day he thought about reasons he could use to do just that. Partly because he hoped another face-to-face might knock some of the air out of his almost too perfect memory of her. Mostly because he hoped it wouldn't.

Stupid. He knew it was. His recent experiences aside, inviting a woman into his life just now was probably the worst thing he could do.

Carter rolled over in the narrow bed. An ancient clattering fan doing little to cool the hot air in the small, two-bedroom bungalow outside the city.

Then a rancid smell made him draw back. He opened his eyes to stare into the droopy face of the neighbor's old hound that sat next to his bed, watching him expectantly.

"Damn." Carter sat up and grabbed his windup alarm clock. Just after eight-thirty in the morning. "How in the hell did you get in here again, Blue?"

All things being equal, Blue was as much his dog as his neighbor's, but Carter couldn't remember letting him in the house last night. He rubbed his face. Probably he'd left the back door open again. While he'd repaired the screen on the outer door a few days ago, it wouldn't take much for a determined dog to undo his handiwork if he put his mind to it.

Carter pulled on his jeans and walked to the small kitchen. Old Blue had definitely put his mind to it.

The hound's nails clacked against the wood floor as he followed him. He barked once, a half howl that could wake all the neighbors. Of course, at eight-thirty most were probably already up.

"All right, all right. Hush now. I'll get your breakfast in a minute."

The dog's only response was to tilt his head to the side. Which was about as good as it got with him.

Carter washed his face in the kitchen sink and shook out his hands before pouring the last of the sludge in the coffeemaker into a cup and putting it into the microwave. Then he filled the food and water bowls for Blue and took both out to the back porch, where the puddle of slobber the hound would leave behind wouldn't be as much of a nuisance as it was inside.

He stood next to the dog, looking around the three acres of land that had been in his family for more than a hundred years. The property had once been a couple of thousand acres, but after four generations, the parcel had been chopped up many times for inheritance purposes, and much of it sold off, so all that remained was the piece of land around him. And he was all that remained in the area of the original family. The brush was overgrown, fences were in disrepair. If he needed any further proof of that, he just had to look at the horse grazing in the distance. Another animal that belonged to one of his neighbors, this time the one to the west.

The microwave dinged. Carter let himself back into the kitchen, considering Blue's handiwork as he did, and took the cup out, downing half the scalding contents before picking up the single telephone on the wall. He put a call through to the Jacksons to tell them to collect their horse before it wandered off where they wouldn't find it.

"Thanks, Carter," Julia Jackson said after a long sigh. "I'll go right out and collect her. Damn horse. She'll never learn that the grass doesn't taste any better on your side of the fence."

Carter hung up the receiver and downed the rest of the coffee, his gaze drawn to the calendar on the wall. It was one of those given away by insurance companies, the pictures horrible, the paper already yellow although it was only August. But it showed the days and that was all that mattered.

Carter looked to where his right hand still rested on the telephone receiver. Then, before he knew he was going to do it, he picked it back up and dialed a number he'd memorized two months ago.

"Gavin, Ewing and Clairmont, Attorneys," a receptionist said in a cheery voice that set Carter's teeth on edge.

"Yeah. Give me Laney Cartwright."

2

LANEY CARTWRIGHT GAZED OUT her tenth-floor office window. It was lunchtime and Bryan Street bustled with life. Life that would vanish after five when everyone scrambled to their homes in the suburbs, leaving Dallas a ghost town dotted with the few tourists and conventioneers who dared peek outside their hotels.

She hadn't been in the windowed office very long. For the past three years she'd worked in a glorified cubicle on the open floor, one of many associate attorneys competing for a shot at the few offices that went up for grabs. Despite her impeccable résumé, she'd worked long and hard for this promotion to junior firm attorney. Eighty-hour weeks, carrying the load of three, burning the candle at both ends and the middle so that she barely had time to sleep, much less have a personal life.

Maybe that was the reason she'd been preoccupied ever since the legal secretary she shared with two other attorneys told her that a certain Mr. Carter Southard had called that morning to make an appointment. Violet had said there was nothing open, but he'd persisted, saying he needed no more than a couple of minutes and that it was important.

Important.

So Laney had told her to pencil something in during the lunch hour. Seeing Carter would at least keep her from thinking too much about the menacing note she'd received that morning.

Now she swiveled her desk chair away from the window and considered the case file open in front of her. When was the last time she'd had sex?

She twisted her lips. That was it, wasn't it? The fact that her love life had been nonexistent for so long was allowing her to daydream about what it might be like to act on that spark of attraction she'd felt two months ago, even though the jail jumpsuit and unshaven appearance of Carter Southard should have been enough to turn her off.

But it hadn't. Instead, in the first two weeks following their meeting, she found herself drifting off mid-conversation during social dinners and even phone calls, her concentration broken by the brief flash of Carter's strong hands. The granite set of his jaw. The half grin he'd given her when he apparently realized she returned the interest he displayed, however reluctantly.

What was she talking about? The sensation had taken her so much by surprise, there hadn't been a chance for her to be reluctant about anything.

Besides, she wouldn't be seeing him again. So what was the harm in returning his smile, letting him see what she was thinking? Saying without words, "Gee, Carter, another time, another place, you and me might have had a good time together. A very good time, indeed."

Laney swallowed hard, realizing that this was another time. And another place. And she was actually looking forward to seeing if that potential for a good time still existed. Oh, she didn't intend to act on it. But that brief interaction with Carter had been enough to fuel some interesting late-night sessions alone up until…well, even last night.

The intercom button buzzed. Laney picked up the phone. "Yes?"

The forty-five-year-old secretary said, "Your father on line one. He wants to know why you canceled lunch."

"Tell him I have an important meeting."

Silence.

Laney sighed. "I'll talk to him." She pressed the button for the correct line and then leaned back in her chair. "Hi, Daddy."

"Hi, yourself. So what's this I hear you've canceled our lunch today?"

"Sorry about that. A new development on the Mac-Gregor case came up and I've scheduled a strategy lunch to work it out."

Laney didn't lie to her father often. Mostly because he knew her better than anyone and immediately spotted an untruth. He would never go so far as to say it, but the few times she had relied on deception to hide her intentions had always ended with them both knowing where they stood.

She supposed that's what happened when you were

so close. After her mother passed away when she was twelve, Laney and her father had formed a bond that transcended parent and child. He was her best friend.

"What's the development?"

Laney blanched. Exhibit A on why she should never lie to her father.

Of course, he knew everything that was happening with *State v. MacGregor,* the case that had dominated her life for the past two months. The case that had also dominated the local and statewide news media, what with her young client accused of first-degree murder during an armed robbery.

The crime itself wasn't so much what garnered interest. Rather it was the fact that Devon MacGregor came from one of the wealthiest families in Texas.

"I received an interesting note this morning," she said quietly.

"Note?"

Laney hadn't planned on saying anything about it just then, but she figured she would have told her father sooner or later, so she might as well use it to her benefit now.

"Yes. Plain block letters. 'Drop MacGregor. Or else.'"

"Or else what?"

Laney sighed and fished out the note she'd placed in a Ziploc bag from the papers on her desk. "Your guess is as good as mine," she said.

"Have you given it to the police?"

"I have a call in. I was told a detective will stop by sometime this afternoon."

"Good."

There was a brief knock on the door. "Your twelve o'clock is here," Violet said.

Laney felt as if her stomach were full of a thousand butterflies flapping their wings to get out.

"Look, Daddy, people are beginning to arrive for the meeting."

She quickly said her goodbyes, hoping that she wasn't being too transparent, then left both hands on the telephone after she'd hung up.

"Hello again," Carter said from the open doorway.

Laney nearly knocked the receiver from its cradle and she fumbled to right it again.

She looked at the man responsible for her duplicity…and discovered that the hectic sensation she'd experienced two months ago was nothing compared with the one the cleaned-up version of Carter Southard made on her now.

What he wore was nothing special—a denim shirt, jeans and cowboy boots. It was the details that did Laney in. The way his sleeves were rolled up over his corded forearms. The cocky way he stood that pulled his well-worn jeans just so across his groin. The scuffed boots that proved he was a man who didn't wear them just for show, but had earned every last speck of Texas dust fused to the old leather.

In Carter's case, he wore the clothes—the clothes didn't wear him.

She looked up to find him grinning knowingly and

the bottom dropped out of her stomach altogether, freeing the butterflies there.

Oh, boy. It looked as though she was going to have to get used to her father's concerned reaction because she had the feeling that she was going to be doing a whole hell of a lot of lying in the foreseeable future.

3

Oh, yes. This was exactly what Carter was looking for. Laney Cartwright's heated reaction to his appearance would stroke any man's ego; to his, it was a much-needed boost.

It wasn't often his path crossed with women of her class. Just seeing her sitting behind that expensive desk in her navy blue suit, her white-blond hair slicked back into some kind of neat do, baring her pale, elegant neck and what he suspected were real pearls at her delicate lobes—it all spoke of someone used to the better things in life.

Merely looking at her made him feel as if he'd soiled her somehow.

His grin widened. Oh, how he wanted to get her even dirtier still.

Laney looked as if she'd forgotten something and quickly got to her feet. She edged around the desk to face him, wiping her palms on her pencil-thin skirt before extending her right hand. "Where are my manners?" she said with a smile. "Hello, Mr. Southard." She gave his hand a quick shake, but Carter held on to hers a heartbeat longer. "It's good to see you again," she said.

He cocked a brow. "Is it?"

He watched as her initial surprise melted into something much different. Much more dangerous. Although to whom, he couldn't say.

She leaned against the edge of her desk and crossed her arms over her chest, drawing his gaze there and down to the long line of her legs in another pair of naughty high heels. She pursed her pink lips and considered him with the same naked suggestion that he knew was in his eyes.

Huh. A woman who liked a challenge.

While Carter could honestly say he'd never dated anyone with so much schooling, he had dated a woman or two who engaged him on more than a physical level. And Laney looked as if she could easily wipe them from his memory, set a new benchmark for those who would come after her.

She obviously enjoyed the sexual game of cat and mouse, where it was never quite clear who was the cat and who the mouse, with each of them easily sliding into either role to achieve some undefined objective.

Undefined? Carter took in the expression on Laney's beautiful face. Oh, no, there was nothing undefined there. Both of them were in it for the kill.

"Violet said you had something important to discuss?" she asked.

"Mmm. Yes. Important."

He stepped nearer to her, catching the subtle scent of magnolias. She smelled like heaven and he wanted to visit for a while. He reached out and fingered a soft curl that had escaped her do, then met her gaze, moving in closer still. He watched with a mixture of amusement and fascination as her pupils dilated in her blue, blue eyes. He guessed she wasn't used to such bold moves, and he liked that he'd still managed to knock her slightly off-kilter. Although he didn't expect her to remain that way for long.

He lowered his chin and then brought it up slowly, making it evident that he was smelling her…and that he liked what he found. The top of his nose brushed against her cheek and she gasped slightly.

He stepped back, holding her gaze captive with his. "I'm a man who always honors his debts and I've come to pay mine."

Laney blinked. "Debt…oh." She appeared to have momentarily forgotten the circumstances of their first meeting. "All expenses surrounding your release have been taken care of."

"Too vague. Who took care of the debt, Laney?"

"Mr. Armstrong."

"And your connection to him would be?"

"Client."

"Strictly?"

She smiled. "I don't see how that impacts the situation, Mr. Southard."

"Carter, please." He was tempted to press his thigh between her legs, force her skirt up and pin her against that expensive desk of hers right there before the window. But he planned to drag the hot anticipation out as long as he could.

Besides, he wasn't sure how far he could push her before she picked up the phone and called for security.

"Answer my question," he insisted. "Brother?"

A corner of her mouth turned up. "Cousin."

"Judging from your name, I'm guessing your mother's side?" He cleared his throat. "Unless Cartwright is your married name."

The other side of her mouth edged up until she was nearly smiling. "My mother's side."

He enjoyed the way she answered the question without answering the question.

Was she married? She wore no ring, but he'd met plenty of women who didn't. Whether it was a barmaid trying to encourage better tips from customers who thought she was single and therefore free game, or a taxi driver who didn't want to risk losing her ring at gunpoint, there were all sorts of reasons why women chose not to advertise their marital status.

Of course, a woman like Laney Cartwright wouldn't want to promote it because the less you knew about her, the better leverage she had.

Carter looked forward to compromising that power in every way that he could.

Laney seemed to realize that the scales were tipped a little too heavily in his favor. So he wasn't surprised when she walked back to the other side of her desk, breaking eye contact with him.

He half expected her to end the meeting. To give up the ghost and realize that indulging in a sexual duel with him benefited her not at all. Instead, she said, "I was about to head for lunch. Would you like to join me?"

He squinted at her.

She pressed the intercom button before he responded. "Violet? Have Raphael's ready a table for two for lunch, please."

And just like that the scales tipped back to her.

LANEY GREETED the maître d' with a kiss to both cheeks, as if seeing an old friend. Which, in essence, she was, since she took so many of her meals at the exclusive French restaurant.

"Miss Laney, how especially beautiful you look today. I was afraid I would not see you after your secretary called earlier to cancel your luncheon plans."

Pierre darted glances Carter's way, as if half hoping that during the conversation Carter would disappear.

"I have your favorite table all ready for you, Ms. Cartwright."

Laney swept her hand toward Carter. "Pierre, this is Mr. Southard. He'll be dining with me today."

She didn't need to say more. Pierre looked as if someone had just hit him in his snobbish head with a two-foot-long salami. And Carter stared back at him as if he didn't know whether to greet Pierre or hit him. He appeared prepared for both.

Laney hid her smile as Pierre explained to Carter that the restaurant had a dress code and asked if he wouldn't mind choosing a suitable jacket from an array they had in the cloakroom.

Laney twisted her lips, pretending that she didn't notice Carter's discomfort while challenging him to react in the way he'd like to. Namely, storm out of the uptight place.

Instead, he motioned for Pierre to lead the way.

Moments later, he came out wearing a bright green blazer bearing the crest of an exclusive club on the breast pocket and a bright yellow tie. Laney couldn't help laughing behind her hand. Not just at the garish combination, but at Pierre's chagrin and Carter's wide grin.

Pierre appeared exasperated as he led them to a table to the left, away from the kitchen and in front of the window, but he could do nothing as he watched Carter take the seat smack-dab where anyone passing could see him.

"Thank you, Pierre," Laney said after he pulled out the other chair for her.

He usually thanked her back or at the very least told her to enjoy her lunch. This time, he just gave her a little bow and then scurried away as fast as his fashionably decked feet could carry him.

The waiter came immediately, not indicating one way or another whether Carter's purposely chosen attire affronted him as he offered the wine list. Carter didn't bother reading it but handed it back and requested a beer in a frosted glass.

Laney did the same.

"I'm impressed," she said quietly, fingering the rim of her water glass and ignoring the stares from neighboring tables. "I figured you would have turned and left the instant Pierre informed you that you weren't dressed properly."

"Then it takes little to impress you."

She enjoyed it when people acted contrary to her expectations. So few did. She could usually predict exactly what a person would say. And was disappointed when they did. So when she came across the odd man like Carter, she liked to linger in his company. Just to see what he would do next.

The waiter served their beer and then informed them of the specials. Laney didn't have to look at the menu he handed her. She already knew every dish listed and what she would have. She was surprised when Carter didn't bother to open his menu, either, instead holding her gaze as the waiter finished with the specials and looked to her.

She ordered salmon with rice and then raised her brow when it was Carter's turn. He didn't even blink as he said, "Give me a strip steak, grilled. Baked potato and salad with vinegar and oil. No gravies, no funny stuff I can't identify. Just give it to me straight up."

The waiter bowed slightly, took back the menus and disappeared.

If Laney had hoped to outmaneuver him by bringing him here, she'd failed. And she couldn't have been happier.

"So," she said, taking a sip of her water, "how is it that you know my cousin Trace?"

Carter grimaced and looked around the nicely appointed room, giving a small finger salute to an older woman nearby who openly stared at him. "He shot me."

Laney nearly spewed her water over the table. "Pardon me?"

Carter's grin returned. "I said he shot me." He formed a gun with his fingers and pulled the trigger. "I have to say that if our positions had been reversed, I'd have done the same thing to him. But I would have hit him so he wouldn't get back up."

Laney had heard stories about her mother's side of the family. "A bunch of rowdy cowboys," her father would say before launching into a story about rustled cattle or gunfights or land feuds involving the branch of her family that came from the southwest part of the state.

Blake Cartwright was never flippant when telling the tales that had undoubtedly grown longer and longer over the years. Rather, he usually looked envious of a way of life so different from his own upbringing chasing oil with his father. Although occasionally guns had been involved, there had been no real honor in any of the clashes. All the disputes had revolved around money and who would be walking away with it. And it was usually Laney's grandfather.

Which explained why Laney had never had to worry about anything. She could have attended the best Ivy League colleges in the world, but had instead chosen to go to the University of Texas. Her father had been proud of the move, when she had expected him to argue with her.

Then again, her father had never acted the way she anticipated, either. Much like the man across from her.

Their salads arrived.

"To be honest with you, Ms. Cartwright—"

"Laney, please."

"Any outstanding debt is only part of the reason why I requested to see you today."

She folded a few spinach leaves onto her fork with the aid of her knife. "Oh?"

Carter took a bite of his salad, and then wiped his mouth with his napkin, resting his elbow on the table as he chased the greens with water. "Christ, they're feeding me cow food. I feel like I should be grazing."

She laughed.

He pushed his plate away and took a bread roll instead, slathering it with butter. Laney found her gaze riveted as he put the extra large bite into his mouth, chewing without much regard for etiquette. A man who was obviously hungry for more than what was on the table in front of him.

"I want you to help get me reinstated into the Corps."

4

"I DON'T NORMALLY HANDLE military cases," Laney had told him when they'd walked back to her office building a couple of blocks away from the restaurant.

"Define 'normally.'"

"Never."

Carter had figured as much. He was already working with a JAG attorney and understood the way the military worked. Especially in his case, after he'd been diagnosed with post-traumatic stress disorder, essentially a rubber stamp they used to cover every personnel problem they encountered. Mouth off to a rookie captain who couldn't tell his ass from an IED—improvised explosive device—and find yourself suspended for an amount of time to be determined by other glorified civilians who were even more clueless than the ones who had diagnosed him in the first place. Men who had no idea what it was to spend days on end in a shit-ridden sandbox without supplies and adequate protection, where everyone and no one could be your enemy, where ultimately your only friends were your weapon and your balls.

Things were just going far too slow for his liking.

Still, Laney had agreed to look into his case. See if there was something she could do to help expedite matters.

Sweat dripped from Carter's forehead, landing on the tile of his kitchen floor where he was on this second set of one hundred push-ups. Old Blue lay nearby, his head on his paws, his droopy eyes shifting up and then down as he followed Carter's movements.

It was after dark and outside the cicadas were kicking up a ruckus as they claimed the night.

This was Carter's least favorite time of day. Darkness yawned in front of him like a murky, endless ditch that no amount of dirt in the world could fill in, no matter how hard he shoveled. Shadows claimed the corners of the small, old house and lengthened, the few lamps and lightbulbs stopping them from swallowing the rooms altogether.

Carter usually did one of two things right about now. Either he sat in front of the old television set with a twelve-pack next to one ankle while Blue rested against the other. Or he hit a nearby roadhouse, seeking temporary companionship and ultimately escape in a welcoming woman's arms.

Neither option seemed palatable to him just now. Mostly because the only arms he could seem to concentrate on belonged to Laney Cartwright.

His muscles trembled as he pushed them beyond their limits. He finally collapsed to the floor, his cheek resting against the cool tile, his lungs on fire. But he paid attention to nothing outside the image of Laney's surprised and happy smile earlier at the restaurant when she realized he wasn't going anywhere.

The closest he'd come to meeting his match in a woman was JoEllen Atchison. He winced. At least that's what he liked to tell himself. It turned out JoEllen must not have returned the sentiment or else she would never have believed him capable of trying to rape her two months ago. Still, before then, he'd been convinced that they had been simpatico, two jarheads who didn't require foreplay but went straight to the deed when the need hit, their only real relationship being with the U.S. Marine Corps.

Carter rolled over and stared at the ceiling. Now with the wisdom that came with hindsight, he realized that what he and JoEllen had had was nothing but a handful of one-night stands that had occasionally included a weekend locked away in a seedy motel room with a box of pizza and a case of beer. And that somewhere down the line he had mistaken that for a relationship.

Of course, it was hard to understand the difference, because he had never really had a steady relationship with a woman. When he was younger, he'd been too busy being a Marine commander's son. There had been no real time for the usual teenage stuff outside his positions as varsity football cornerback and team captain, the roles nothing more to him than warm-up for what he would do once he enlisted in the Marines when he was eighteen.

Girls…oh, they'd been there. Lifting up their pretty

skirts and kissing him with their cherry-flavored lip gloss. But he'd never seen one of them more than three times, and even then not necessarily in a row, since he went out with other girls in between. He hadn't fooled himself into thinking that the reason he got away with such bad behavior had to do with his good looks. As his father had liked to tell him, he looked two licks shy of a full tongue bath.

No, he knew his status as football captain allowed him certain privileges. Liberties he hadn't been extended in the Corps, where one Marine was treated no different than a hundred others.

His mother…well, his mother lived down in Austin with another family. One she'd started after leaving Carter with his father when he was five, marrying another man and going on to have four more children that were no more like Carter than the sun was like the moon.

Heaving himself up from the floor, he opened the refrigerator, staring at the half-dozen bottles of beer in there, and reached for the water bottle instead. Unscrewing the top, he went to stand at the back doorway, staring out at the dark sky as he guzzled a good portion of cold water.

It wasn't often that he wondered how life would have turned out for him had his mother taken him with her instead of leaving him with his father. Only every now and again when he found himself drifting in a sea of uncertainty. As he was now.

Would he have been a lawyer like Laney? A doctor?

All four of his half siblings either boasted advanced degrees or were in the process of earning them.

Instead, the reason his mother had left his father had become a way of life for Carter, as well: the Corps.

And he had holes in his stomach knowing that they no longer wanted him.

Blue whined at his feet. Carter looked down at the old hound licking his drooping chops.

"What is it, boy?" He lifted the water bottle. "You want some of this?"

He opened the back door and led the way out onto the porch, where he poured a good portion into the dog's bowl. The hound lapped it up.

Carter dropped to sit on the edge of the small landing, letting his feet dangle over the side. On the kitchen table his M16 assault rifle lay partially disassembled where he'd been cleaning it, next to a half-eaten burger he'd picked up from a nearby diner earlier.

He spotted the waxing quarter moon rising from the other side of the trees and thought again of Laney Cartwright. Wondered what she was doing right about then.

Wondered if she was thinking about him.

LANEY LAY BACK against the down pillows piled up against her headboard, her feet tucked under the soft Egyptian cotton sheets because they always got cold with the air conditioner on. The grandfather clock her father had bought her a couple of years ago chimed the hour in the front room of her two-bedroom penthouse apartment as she leafed through the MacGregor case file, trying to figure out who might want to threaten her. Laughter caught her attention and she looked up to try to catch the joke she'd just missed on her DVD of the third season of *Sex and the City*. It wasn't long before her wandering attention wandered farther still and she was thinking about Carter Southard and the time they'd spent together earlier in the day.

So Carter Southard was a Marine.

She didn't know why she was surprised. He fit all the physical requirements of the job. And certainly the mental criteria, as well.

Still, somehow she imagined him doing something else. Say, drilling for oil. Or running a cattle ranch. Something that required him to be out in the sun all day toiling away.

Of course, he could do that as a Marine, but…

She sighed. Okay, her thoughts were veering toward the ridiculous. All because she was trying to ignore the fact that she was so enormously attracted to him she'd nearly blown off her afternoon agenda on the MacGregor case and called him. Not for social reasons. But to get the name of his JAG attorney, which he'd promised to supply.

Not for social reasons, indeed.

Although that wasn't far off the mark. She didn't want to take him to a garden party or a symphony bene-fit. She wanted to share her bed with him.

Laughter caught her attention again and she forced herself to look down at the file resting against the easel formed by her knees. She should be thinking about the brief meeting she'd had with a police detective after lunch. About his questions on the MacGregor case and who might want to send her the threatening note. But she hadn't been able to help him. MacGregor hadn't had an accomplice. He was being charged as the lone gunman in a convenience store robbery that had left a male clerk dead.

So who would want to warn her off the case?

Well, she certainly wasn't going to solve the mystery tonight. Not with her mind wandering to Carter every two seconds.

She closed the file and put it on the bedside table, then reached for the bottle of lotion there, smoothing a good squirt over her arms and knees before sliding farther down under the sheets.

"Do you make a habit of picking up strays?" Carter had asked her as they'd walked back to the office after lunch.

"What?"

He'd shrugged. "I can't help wondering if taking on strange cases is something you do on a regular basis, or if I'm the exception."

She'd stopped in front of the building and faced him, watching the way he squinted against the midday sun, causing fine lines to fan out from his granite eyes.

"Oh, you're definitely an exception, Carter Southard," she'd said. "And I have the feeling that this isn't the only rule you're going to inspire me to break."

Laney found herself smiling faintly at the memory.

It was more than Carter's unpredictability that engaged her; it was also the way she felt when she was around him. In a life full of dull days, he'd lit a fire she couldn't help being drawn to.

But if he'd been strictly fantasy material before, now he was very real.

She found that her hand had made its way down the silk of her nightgown, sliding over her hip bone and then back up again. Just thinking about him made her feel sexy, alive. Merely knowing that all she had to do was pick up the phone and make what her friends termed a "booty call" and he'd be over made her feel naughty for even considering it.

She bit her bottom lip. God, the way she was reacting to him, you'd think she was a virgin locked away from the world for the first twenty-eight years of her life. Not a woman who'd experienced her share of orgasms, although not as often as she'd like. Sue her, but she'd yet to find a man capable of supplying her with more than one or two. Usually after a couple of dates, the men either wanted to start staying over or wanted her to sleep at their place. And she hadn't been interested in either.

That, or they'd expected her to fawn over them, turning from a no-nonsense, ambitious attorney to a woman who could think of nothing else but making them happy, a woman with nothing but wedding dates and dinner parties on her mind.

It didn't take long for them to figure out that she didn't fit into the normal Southern girl mold. At least not yet, her father occasionally liked to joke, reminding her that time had a way of changing even the strongest, career-minded women.

She couldn't imagine herself changing, ever.

Still, even she admitted to pain when she'd spot her most recent ex with another woman. He'd make sure to introduce her to his latest conquest, who appeared to be just up his alley.

Carrie Bradshaw made a quip about men that normally would have amused her. Now she reached for the remote and shut off the television, then turned off the light, wondering if the rest of the world was out of sync with her. Or if she was out of sync with the world.

5

"SO, TELL ME. Who is he?" Blake Cartwright asked.

Laney was suddenly incapable of swallowing the thinly sliced beef in her mouth. It had been two days since she'd lunched at Raphael's with Carter. Still, that didn't stop her from glancing toward the table she had sat at with him, barely seeing the older couple now lunching there.

She drank deeply from her water glass to help the food go down. "Pardon me?"

Blake pointed at her with his fork. "No pardon granted." He took a bite of his trout and then put his utensils down and dabbed at his mouth with his napkin. Her father was so different from Carter in that he'd eaten at this and similar restaurants hundreds of times and proper protocol was second nature to him. His suit was tailored, his shirt snow-white and freshly starched, his tie silk and pierced with a clip, his hair neatly trimmed. But his question and follow-up response proved that he had more in common with Carter when it came to seeing through her.

He narrowed his gaze. "You've been distracted ever since you came in. By now I usually know as many details about your latest case as your associates do, as well as what you've had for dinner the night before."

Laney's mouth dropped open. Thankfully there was nothing in it to fall out. "I can't possibly talk all that much."

Her father's grin warmed her. "Maybe not all that much. But enough for me to know today's quiet is out of character."

Laney readjusted her napkin in her lap. "I'm just a little distracted, is all. I went to see MacGregor at the county jail this morning before today's hearing." She gave a slight shiver, always uncomfortable with her visits to places where iron bars were the dominant décor. "He has no idea who might have sent me that note."

"Have you heard from the detective you gave it to?"

"Yes. No fingerprints. No unique characteristics."

"No reason to further pursue the matter."

"His words exactly."

Her father folded his hands on the edge of the table. "Would you like me to look into it?"

Blake Cartwright had had big shoes to fill, following Laney's legendary grandfather. But he had never really looked at it that way. Perhaps once he might have, but that would have been long before Laney was old enough to notice. Most men with inherited wealth were happy to accept a token role in the family business, allowing their money to make money for them. Not her father. He wanted to leave his own unique mark. And he was doing just that by establishing himself as a very successful venture capitalist.

In the past ten years alone, Laney could count fifteen of his schemes that had taken off, adding significantly to his wealth, most of them in green technology. Of course, he'd had to invest in a hundred to score on those fifteen, and she'd enjoyed hearing about every one of them, including the wacky idea of a hat that allowed advertisers to buy space on it when the owner registered with the mother Web site.

Laney realized her father was waiting for an answer, so she shook her head. "Thanks, but no. I don't feel I'm at any great risk."

"Sounds like famous last words to me."

She smiled. "God, I hope not. I didn't get into this line of work to put my life at risk. If I had wanted to do that, I would have become a police officer."

"Honest work."

"Honest work that gets you shot in the ass."

Blake laughed loudly and sat back, oblivious to the looks he got. "You know, you never did answer my question."

"What question?" She pretended an interest in finishing her meal.

"You know very well what question. I heard you were in here with another man the other day. You know, the one when you canceled your luncheon date with me so you could conduct an emergency meeting on the MacGregor case."

Laney frowned. "How could I forget how small this big city can be?"

How stupid! She should have known that word would get back to her father. Especially considering the interest that Carter had garnered. There were probably people in the room even now whom she might not know personally but who knew her father. And while none of them would openly gossip about Carter's questionable appearance (it wasn't the Texan thing to do), they would politely ask after him in a way that would get their unspoken meaning across.

"So are you planning to tell me?" her father asked again.

Laney shook her head. "No. Because he's of no concern."

And he wasn't, was he? At least not to her father. She hadn't heard from Carter since that day and was beginning to accept the fact that she might not. Which meant that there was zero chance that she'd ever introduce him to her father.

She caught herself wistfully fingering the hair at the nape of her neck and stopped, smiling at her father, who watched her curiously.

"I see," he said.

She opened her mouth to ask him what he saw, then thought better of it. She knew not to ask her father anything she wasn't ready to hear the answer to.

"Anyway, my love life is dismally boring compared to yours," she said, lobbing the conversation back in his direction.

His expression shifted as if to say, "That's more like

it," and he chuckled. "At least you're admitting to having a love life."

She didn't. But despite Carter's silence, she held out a slim hope that might change.

LANEY USUALLY TOOK the McKinney Avenue tram back and forth to work. It was convenient and fast. But in this heat, it also meant that she'd be soaked with sweat before she got to the office. So she'd taken to driving.

If her new habit had anything to do with the threatening note she'd received, she wasn't saying.

Besides, if she didn't drive to work, when else would she get to enjoy her Infiniti hybrid? The luxury vehicle was designed to please, and she liked being behind the wheel, feeling in control of her world as the city buildings loomed outside her windows.

She pressed the elevator button to take her to the garage level and then looked at her watch. After seven. Most everyone else in the company had gone home for the day. As usual, she'd let time get away from her while working out the MacGregor defense, and when she'd finally looked up, the sun was a huge, orange ball on the western horizon.

The bell dinged and the elevator doors opened. She stepped out, her footsteps echoing in the nearly empty chamber. She slowed, giving a little shiver and gripping her briefcase more tightly. If need be, she could use it as a weapon.

She rolled her eyes and took a deep breath. And just

who, exactly, was she expecting to accost her? The janitor with a broom demanding she hand over her thousand-dollar Jimmy Choos?

She was tired, that's all. And the lack of sleep was amplifying the fear that lingered in the wake of that threatening note. She didn't have anything to worry about. She hadn't committed any crime. Wronged anyone else. She was merely defending her innocent client.

And she did believe that Devon MacGregor was innocent, didn't she? While she didn't think she was an expert, she considered herself a pretty good judge of human behavior. And Devon MacGregor's pleas for her to believe him and the supporting, if meager, evidence told her that her client had been wrongfully accused.

Which meant that the real culprit was still out there somewhere.

God. Of course. That was it. Whoever had committed the crimes was probably very interested in letting Devon serve the time for them.

The thought had crossed her mind before, but she'd dismissed it. She wasn't interested in pointing the finger at anyone else, merely turning the fingers pointing at her client away from him.

The elevator dinged and she jumped.

Okay, she really needed to get a grip.

Still, she looked over her shoulder, watching to see who got out.

No one did.

The elevator doors slid shut again.

Now, that wasn't a figment of her imagination. That was just downright creepy.

Palming her key ring, she picked up her pace. Only a hundred feet separated her from her car. She kept to the middle of the floor, away from shadowy pillars, her gaze darting around for any activity. At this time of day there was none. Her quickened footsteps seemed to taunt her. She considered lightening her footfalls so she could hear if there were others. At this rate, she wouldn't hear a car engine above the sound of her own heartbeat.

She turned the corner and someone stepped out of the shadows. She cried out and swung her briefcase, simultaneously trying to figure out the safest escape route. The stranger was between her and her car, so that was out. It was a long way back to the elevator and the stairs. The closest route was the spiraling ramp leading out onto the street.

"Whoa."

A man's voice. A familiar man's voice.

She stared into Carter Southard's handsomely surprised face when he righted himself after ducking.

"Jesus," Laney said, leaning her hand against the trunk of her car. "What are you trying to do? Scare the spirits out of me?"

He reached out and took her briefcase from her other hand, setting it closer to the car door. "Was that the best you could do? Swing your bag?"

Laney managed to get her breathing under control

and stood straight. "You mean you were deliberately trying to frighten me? To see what I would do?"

He grinned. "No. I wasn't. But in hindsight, I suppose my stepping out like that probably wasn't the smartest move."

"You can say that again."

"I think once is enough."

"Funny. Very funny." Laney rubbed her arms. "What are you doing here, anyway?"

He tucked his hands into his front jeans pockets. "I wanted to get you that information I promised. Sorry it's so late. But I told my neighbor that I'd help him repair his fence. Turned into a two-day job and I just finally knocked off." He glanced toward the elevator. "I figured you as the workaholic type, so I thought it was a pretty good bet you'd still be here. And since the lobby was closed, this was my best chance for entry."

"Yes, well," she said, looking around at shadows that didn't seem as sinister with Carter at her side. "I'll have to have a talk with management about this."

"Might be a good idea. At least they could make sure the parking attendant doesn't think sleeping with his feet up on the counter is part of his job description."

"How did you know this was my car?"

"Educated guess." He gestured toward the luxury vehicle. "But that's not what drew me over this way. I'd planned to come up to the office."

She grimaced at him as he stepped to the side, revealing the flat front tire.

"Great," she said, exasperated, wondering if her auto service could gain access to the garage.

"That wouldn't be so bad," Carter said, "if the other tire wasn't flat, too. One flat tire, fate. Two? Someone wanted to make it difficult for you to get home tonight."

Laney slowly walked toward the front of the car, considering the damage.

"See that," Carter said, pointing to the sidewall. "Looks like a knife slash."

Laney shuddered, feeling as if a knife-wielding stranger was in front of her instead of long gone.

"What's this?" she said.

She leaned forward, spotting a note under the wiper, not unlike the one she'd received in the mail a couple of days ago. She pulled it out.

"Drop the MacGregor case. Now." Next to the words was the number two.

"That doesn't look good to me," Carter said, his voice low and gravelly. "That doesn't look good to me at all."

6

AN HOUR LATER, the police had come and gone, assuring her that the detective who had taken her earlier report would be informed of the latest development; Laney's tires had been replaced by her auto service, and Carter stood facing her once again, blessedly alone. And without a briefcase being swung at his head.

He resisted the desire to reach out and push back a few strands of errant hair. Aw, hell, who was he kidding? He'd never been the best at restraint, and he saw no real benefit in starting now. She appeared shaken, in need of protection. Yet just under the surface shone hard steel, telling him that she was much stronger than she looked. It would take more, much more, than a couple of threatening notes to knock her over.

Laney looked down but didn't pull away as he rubbed the baby-soft strands of her hair between his thumb and forefinger. Then he brushed them away from her milky cheek and tucked them behind her ear, wondering at the delicate shell and the sight of his dark hand against her light skin.

"Thanks for staying," she said quietly. "I really appreciate it." She briefly bit the side of her bottom lip and looked around, apparently still seeing ghosts. "But if it's all the same to you, I'd prefer not to spend another minute more than I have to in this garage."

Carter smiled. "I understand." He gestured to his bike. "Let me follow you home."

"That's not necessary," she said a little too quickly, then her gaze lingered on his. "Really, it isn't. I don't think I'll be finding another note tonight." She looked into the cavernous depths of the garage. "At least I hope not."

"I'd feel better if I saw you home. Where do you live?"

She told him. He raised a brow at the downtown address. He'd expected something in one of the swanky Texas subdivisions. Not that Dallas didn't boast more than a few high-rent condos downtown, but somehow he figured her for an estate development.

"Apartment building?" he asked.

She nodded.

"Front doorman?"

"Yes. And closed-circuit cameras and the latest in security."

That made him feel better. At least marginally. "Good. But let's get you there first. Have you had anything to eat?"

"What? Um, no."

He opened the driver's door of her car, indicating that she should climb in.

"Lead the way," he said.

WOULD HE WANT to come in? Laney wondered. Did she dare invite him up?

Her palms grew damp against the steering wheel. The classical station her car radio was tuned in to was failing to capture her attention. She drifted into the opposite lane twice since she was more focused on watching Carter in her rearview mirror than on the road in front of her.

Only an hour ago, she had thought he was gone from her life, that he had no plan to follow up on his request for help. Then he'd appeared out of nowhere, nearly scaring the socks off her.

Now he was following her on his Harley, looking particularly hot in his snug black T-shirt and sunglasses, his longish dark hair blowing in the wind. Knowing a bit about his military background, he could have been out for a ride or on his way to the front line.

The thought of him looking after her like this made her hot, and she squeezed her thighs together.

When was the last time she'd felt this way? Had she ever felt this way? She couldn't say. What she did know was that none of the suited, professional men she'd briefly dated over the past couple of years had made her mouth go this dry. And her heart beat in an uneven rhythm in her chest at the thought that the man on the motorcycle wanted her.

Of course, part of her response could be attributed to her tires being slashed. The violent act had opened her eyes to the seriousness of the threat in a way the first note had not.

Still, she couldn't think about that now. She seemed utterly incapable of thinking about anything but the man behind her.

She pulled in front of her apartment building and began to roll down her window. To thank him or invite him up—she wasn't sure which. Instead, he took the decision out of her hands by offering a brief wave and roaring down the street.

Interesting…

Okay, maybe this unpredictability wasn't as attractive as she'd first thought. She'd never considered he would merely drive off.

Laney watched the back of his bike. Despite her disappointment, she couldn't help thinking he looked as good going as he did coming. She reluctantly got out of her car, deciding to ask the doorman to arrange for the Infiniti to be parked in the underground garage. She didn't have the stomach right now to do it herself.

A short time later, she'd showered and was in her robe in her penthouse apartment, considering the contents of her refrigerator, when the apartment intercom buzzed.

"Yes, Roger?" she asked the front doorman.

There was a pause, making her wonder if something else had happened.

"Sorry to bother you, Ms. Cartwright, but there's a Mr. Southard here to see you."

Roger's pause hadn't been reluctance to share bad news, but grudging acceptance that he'd have to introduce a man who must look incredibly out of place in the upscale lobby.

Laney swallowed hard. Carter had come back?

"Ms. Cartwright?"

"What? Oh. Yes. Yes, Roger. Send him right up."

"Very good, miss."

Laney rushed toward her bedroom to put something on, but there wasn't time for that. So she rushed back and collected her shoes and jacket from the floor and chair near the door and tossed both into the closet. She'd just closed the door when the bell rang. She leaned against the wall for a few moments, taking deep breaths. Then she affixed a smile to her face and opened the front door.

"Hope you like anchovies," Carter said, entering with a box of pizza and a six-pack of beer.

OH, WHEN LANEY OPENED the door, she'd tried to act as if everything were all right. But Carter knew better. She'd been shaken by the incident in the parking garage more than she would admit.

Not that he could blame her. The office neighborhood wasn't the type where random tire slashings by juveniles were a regular occurrence. Besides, juveniles didn't normally leave threatening notes behind.

Laney had told him that this was the second such note. Not that she'd had to. Both her reaction to it, and the number two written on it, had told him as much.

He didn't make it a point to keep up with local news. He watched it, but absorbed very little beyond the weather report. If rain was forecast, he had to put away his bike and take out the old pickup he sometimes drove. But when she told him the threats were connected to the MacGregor case, he knew what she was referring to. He had seen the broadcast videos of the kid in the mask robbing the convenience store and shooting the clerk, who had already handed over the money, his death meaningless. The grainy footage had been run no more than a dozen times the night it was released to the media.

Laney had excused herself after putting the pizza on the counter that separated the kitchen from the living room and the beer in the fridge, and had emerged from what he guessed was her bedroom in a pair of snug white slacks and clingy top. The same color that was everywhere he looked.

He wished she had stayed in the short, white silk robe. Then again, if she had, he probably wouldn't have had the fortitude to sit talking with her at the counter, but would have given in to the desire to ravish her in five minutes flat.

He watched with a raised brow as she polished off her third piece of pizza and chased it with the rest of her second beer.

She seemed to read his thoughts and stopped chewing. It took her a moment to swallow what was in her mouth. "Oh my God. I'm a pig."

He'd figured she hadn't been paying much attention as she talked. About nothing in particular and everything in general.

"I'm going to have to call my trainer to come an extra day this week."

"Trainer?"

She put another piece of pizza on his plate and then wiped her hands. "Yes. Travis. He comes over at six in the morning three days a week to help me work out."

Carter wasn't sure how he felt about a man being around her for that much time, much less getting to see her sweat.

"Usually he takes me running, and then we stop by the gym up the street where he works out a strength training routine."

He gave her a once-over. That would certainly explain why she was so slender and fit. And he fully admitted the desire to see exactly how fit. Without the too-white clothes she wore.

Carter took a swig from his bottle and looked around the place. The penthouse. He wasn't surprised. He'd pretty much nailed Ms. Laney Cartwright's entitled background from the instant he laid eyes on her. And everything he'd seen since only confirmed that.

"Been here long?" he asked.

"Three years. No, wait. Four."

"I take it you like white?"

She laughed. "Daddy's house has always been such a bachelor pad—dark paneling, dark leather furniture—that I couldn't wait to get my own place and lighten things up."

Ah, a daddy's girl. "Bachelor?"

"Mmm. My mom died when I was twelve. He's been

single ever since." She smiled as she absently folded her napkin. "He says that's because he was afraid I'd chase off any other woman, but it's not true. I can't even remember him bringing anyone home."

"And now?"

She threaded her fingers through curls that were soft and white blond and then leaned her head against the heel of her hand. "My, aren't you the curious one."

She had no idea.

"As for Daddy…I guess you could say that we're both kind of serial daters."

Now that her mind was no longer on the pizza and she'd emptied her head of all the apparently random information floating around there, she grew still. Too still. And focused on him with a laser intensity.

She was sexy when she was eating.

She was drop-dead gorgeous when she was looking at him like she was now. As if she wanted to eat him.

Carter cleared his throat and eyed the piece of pizza. He suspected he wouldn't be able to swallow a bite. His jeans were already growing unbearably tight. And the desire to kiss Laney's decadent mouth was growing right along with other strategic areas.

"So…" Laney practically purred, crossing her legs.

Carter watched the way she wrapped one leg around the other, rubbing the top of her bare foot against her other calf.

"So, admit it. Now that I'm acting like a damsel in distress, you're looking to take advantage."

"The thought had crossed my mind."

But he was battling it for all he was worth. A woman had caused him all sorts of trouble two months ago. He wasn't in the market for that kind of trouble again. At least not so soon.

Before he knew that's what he was going to do, he'd grabbed her hips and hauled her so that she was sitting on top of the counter in front of him. He swept the pizza box and beer bottles off to the side.

So much for good intentions.

Laney gasped, apparently surprised by his actions. And pleased, if her sparkling, provocative eyes and catlike grin were any indication.

If they weren't, the way she positioned her feet on either side of his hips was.

"Mmm," Laney hummed, her pupils growing large. "I would never have guessed."

Carter tightened his hands on her hips, raking his gaze over her beautiful face, down to her breasts and farther still to the vee of her crotch.

"I'd say you have a lot to learn about me, then," he said as he leaned in and finally sampled the mouth that had been driving him crazy since the first time he'd laid eyes on it.

7

FOR REASONS SHE COULDN'T QUITE put her finger on, Laney felt as if she'd just taken a deep breath of air, and when she exhaled, all the anxiety and uneasiness connected with the tire slashing were gone. A languid, almost intoxicating responsiveness flowed through her, making her überaware of Carter wedged between her thighs.

Thighs that were clothed and yearning to be otherwise.

Laney entwined her fingers in his hair, finding it slightly curly as it grew out of what was probably a crew cut. With any other man, she might have found Carter's spontaneous action a bit too forward. But not with him. She knew on a fundamental level that they'd been building toward this from the moment they first met. And there was a breathless beauty in allowing it to unfold naturally.

Carter squeezed her hips, pressing her more insistently against his hardness. Laney licked her lips even as she eyed his full mouth, mere inches away from hers.

"You seem awfully confident," she whispered.

His knowing grin made her womanhood throb. "Let's just say I'm an expert when it comes to recon."

He worked his fingers under her top and skimmed his left hand up until the material bunched on her chest. He cupped her breast. She lost the ability to draw a breath.

"And what does your fact-finding mission prove?"

The rough pad of his thumb flicked over her taut nipple through the fabric of her bra. "That you're very amenable to any...invasion I might like to stage."

Laney shifted, the tension curling in her stomach nearly unbearable as he tunneled his fingers under her bra cup. "And do you?"

He reached around and easily popped her bra catch, causing the material to slip forward, leaving her semibare to his gaze. "Do I what?"

"Want to stage an invasion?"

His focus shifted from her breasts to her face. "I want to conquer everything in my sight."

Laney brazenly challenged him. "So what's stopping you?"

Later, she wouldn't be able to recount exactly what had happened. One moment they'd been locked in an unspoken battle of gazes, the next he claimed her mouth completely, plundering the depths with his tongue, demanding a surrender she refused to grant. Instead, she gave back, planning her own line of attack as she reached for his T-shirt and pulled the cotton up over his head. His skin drew tight over well-developed muscles, indicating that he hadn't been exactly sedentary since he'd been released from service. While she'd never dated a slouch, she'd also never dated a man with arguably zero body fat, a mixture of hard steel and pliable skin.

He countered her move by stripping her of her top and bra. But it wasn't until he took her right breast deep into his mouth that she relinquished important ground, incapable of doing anything but closing her eyes and relishing the delicious sensations rippling through her.

He cupped both breasts in his hands, licking and sucking and squeezing. Laney wriggled so her softness pressed more insistently against his hardness. She wanted him more than she wanted to press her advantage. Rather than counter him move for move, she surrendered, for the moment conceding that he might be the better ruler of her body.

And as he stripped her of the last piece of clothing, she was proven very, very right.

LANEY TASTED like ripe Texas peaches generously topped with fresh cream. And Carter's desire to swallow her whole inflated with each kiss and every lick.

He had suspected she'd just showered when she'd opened the door in her robe, but what he was sampling had nothing to do with soap and everything to do with the delectable woman in his arms.

Jesus, she was more beautiful without clothes. Something he didn't come across every day. Lingerie could go a long way toward hiding a woman's flaws. A bra could compensate for small breasts or support saggy ones. But not when it came to Laney. Her snow-white tits sat full and pert, her rosy pink nipples puckered, just begging for the attention he was giving them.

She shifted restlessly against his pulsing erection. He reluctantly ceased ravishing her generous chest and grasped her bare hips, hoisting her to sit back on the counter in front of him. He allowed his gaze to roam over every sweet inch of her. Every soft curve, every shallow hollow. She leaned against her elbows, watching him watch her through heavily lidded eyes. If he could bottle and sell the way he felt in that one moment, he'd be a millionaire a thousand times over.

In fact, he knew a moment of hesitation. Laney was almost too perfect. While he refused to accept that he was socially or mentally lower than her, when you put her brains and beauty together into that phenomenally sexy package…well, she was surely too good for the likes of him.

"Not having second thoughts, are you, Marine?" she whispered, her pink tongue flicking out to slide across her full, kissed red lips.

Was he ever. Not because he didn't want her, but because in that one moment he wanted her too much.

She spread her thighs, boldly baring herself to his gaze.

Carter groaned at the sight of the springy white-blond curls there. If he'd had any doubt as to the genuine color of her hair, he didn't anymore. There was no way this color came out of a bottle.

He couldn't help himself. He had to touch her. Had to see if she tasted as good as she looked.

He slid his fingers down her smooth legs, parting her knees even farther. The rounded mound that was the focus of his attention split slightly, the fleshy outer lips swollen, the inner the same deep pink color as her nipples.

He set his back teeth to keep from taking her right then. Burying himself so deep inside her he was afraid he'd never want to come out.

Instead, with more control than he knew he possessed, he followed the line of her slit with the pads of his thumbs, then opened the protective soft tissue, revealing the tight pearl at the apex. He leaned in and ran his tongue over it.

Laney gasped, her entire body shivering.

Carter fastened his lips around the engorged flesh and suckled it much as he would if he were licking the juice from an oyster.

Laney cried out just as he thrust two fingers deep inside her dripping channel, more to feel her muscles tighten and convulse around him than to draw out the sensations.

Before she could recover, Carter had sheathed himself with a condom he'd freed from his back jeans pocket and parted her farther, positioning the engorged head of his erection against her. He looked at her, giving her one last chance to refuse him.

Instead, she bore down against him, forcing entrance

even as she dropped her head back, her muscles instantly contracting around him again.

Carter was helpless and followed quickly after her.

THE NEXT FEW DAYS, the very air around Laney seemed to be charged with electricity. Everything crackled and popped. Her body hummed, her mind wandered, taking her back to the night before and the white-hot sex she'd had with Carter Southard.

In her entire life, she couldn't remember a time when she felt so aware of herself as a woman. So uninhibited. She'd hungrily taken and unselfishly given, utterly insatiable even after they'd moved their activities to her bedroom.

She must have finally fallen asleep somewhere around three in the morning. She had slept through the 5:00 a.m. phone call from her personal trainer. She didn't wake up until after nine when, finally, the ringing phone caught her attention. It had been Violet from the office, informing her of her lateness.

Of course, Carter had been long gone, having let himself out at some point. She hadn't bothered looking for a note. Didn't need to look for one. There was no way he could have been unmoved by what they'd shared. So she never entertained the thought that she might not see him again.

But now it was Friday afternoon, two days since she'd seen Carter. She was amazed at how quickly the time went by and wondered if she should call him.

She glanced at the file on the corner of her desk. It contained the documents Carter's JAG attorney had faxed over late last night. She'd found them waiting for her when she got in.

She opened the file and read the reason for Carter's suspension: "Subject is reportedly demonstrating extreme symptoms of post-traumatic stress disorder and in his doctor's opinion is close to a psychotic breakdown."

Laney tapped her pencil on her desk. The notation didn't seem at all in line with what she knew about Carter. He showed no signs of PTSD as far as she could tell. Something must be going on for him to be suspended at a time when the military was stretched thin and given that his overall record was impeccable.

Of course, it would be just her luck to fall for a guy who was a closet schizophrenic.

The intercom buzzed. Laney absently reached out to press the button without taking her gaze away from the file in front of her. "What is it, Violet?"

"You wanted me to remind you to visit the Mac-Gregor kid?"

Laney frowned and shifted her watch around her wrist so she could read the face. "Thanks, Violet."

"No problem."

She closed Carter's file and collected the items she needed for her visit to the county jail.

CARTER PACED the sidewalk for the third time, beginning to build up a sweat in the afternoon sun. He knew there was a reason he hated cities. All that damn concrete absorbing the heat like a charcoal briquette and then passing it back to whatever idiot happened to be standing on top of it.

In this case, it was him.

He stopped and looked at the church in front of him. He'd parked his bike a couple of blocks away instead of in the church parking lot. He'd thought the walk would do him good and had hoped that not having access to easy escape would compel him to go inside, rather than back to his bike like the half-dozen other times he'd come here.

Instead, he was being cooked to well done on the damn sidewalk.

"Can I help you?"

Carter turned toward a young man in Marine khakis. He was apparently going inside for the group meeting of PTSD-R-Us and had caught Carter loitering outside.

The kid couldn't be any older than twenty-two, and looked even younger when he grinned, despite the buzz cut and the size of his guns.

"Hey, I'm Matt Starkweather."

Carter eyed the hand the Marine held out. He didn't dare not take it.

"And you are?" the guy asked when he didn't say anything.

"I'm…late for an appointment," he said, pulling his hand back and walking quickly away.

God damn it all to hell. He wouldn't stand a chance

of getting back into the Marines if he didn't attend the group meeting being held in that church. Then why in the hell was he having such a hard time going inside?

Why? Because he didn't have a problem, that's why.

"We'll be here same time tomorrow," Starkweather called out behind him.

Carter threw him a look over his shoulder and grumbled something that may have sounded like a thanks. And then he practically ran to his bike, feeling as if the devil were on his heels.

If it weren't for Laney, he wouldn't have tried to come. But damn fool that he was, he'd gotten up yesterday morning feeling like a new man and had decided it was long past time he did a little work on the old one.

The problem was, the old one was fighting him all the way.

He didn't need help. That's what he'd told all those damn military shrinks over in Afghanistan. And nothing had changed since then. They should be putting him back on the front line where he could do the most good. Being mothballed here in the States wasn't helping anyone. Least of all him.

He got onto his bike and revved the motor, feeling worse than he had since he had been forced onto that transport to come back here.

And the only one who seemed able to make him feel better was Laney.

He pointed his bike in the direction of her office.

8

LANEY STARED at the kid across from her. She couldn't imagine how anyone could think him responsible for the crime he was charged with. But given the evidence against him, she was worried she might not be able to prove his innocence.

He was all of nineteen years old, a UT sophomore majoring in aeronautics. His record was clean outside a couple of minor incidents when he was fourteen involving graffiti and petty theft. Nothing that would indicate him remotely capable of murder one in the armed robbery of a convenience store where there was only sixty-five dollars in the till.

"Devon, you have to tell me who could have done this."

Devon blinked big blue eyes at her. "I have no idea, Laney."

The MacGregors went way back with her family. Laney had even babysat the boy across from her, along with his older sister, a couple of times when she was a teen. Although she hadn't needed to work, it was considered a rite of passage for kids her age. Babysitting was a way to get out of the house and out from under your parents' thumb so you could do what you wanted.

Of course, she'd never felt the need to get away from her father, but she had found she enjoyed babysitting. It was a form of role-playing. Stepping into someone else's life for a few hours, playing mom to their kids, housekeeper to their home. And after the night was through, you got to return to your own life.

And the kids she'd minded had always been good. Including Devon and his sister.

Which was why she hadn't hesitated to take on his case.

She tucked away her notepad. "You do realize that the trial begins a week from Monday?" she asked.

He dropped his chin to his chest. "Yes." He looked back up at her. "But how am I supposed to tell you something I have no way of knowing? All I know is that I did not rob that store that night and kill that guy."

"Then someone is setting you up, Devon. And it's possible you may know who."

He shook his head. "There's no one."

"Fine. Give it some more thought. If anything occurs to you, call my office."

"I will."

She was being threatened, so someone out there was afraid she would find out the truth. But what truth? Or were they afraid she'd get Devon off and have the light shone in another direction? Possibly theirs.

She needed to find out who was behind the threats

before an innocent kid went to jail for a crime he didn't commit.

And before her stalker slashed more than her tires.

She motioned the guard to be let out of the meeting room after saying goodbye to Devon. The door opened and then closed after her as she headed down the hall, pushing her notepad into her purse.

"Oh, hi, Laney."

She looked up to see Devon's sister. "Hi, Darcy. You here to visit Devon?"

The younger woman smiled. "What? Do you think I might know somebody else in here?"

Laney laughed. "You never know." Then it occurred to her that while Devon might not have a clue who was trying to set him up, his sister might. "Wait a minute, Darcy. Do you mind if I talk to you for a bit?"

"Sure. But I don't know how long they'll hold Devon."

"I'll be brief." She put her case down on the hall floor. "Do you have any idea who might want to set up Devon?"

"No. But his girlfriend might."

Girlfriend? Devon had told her he didn't have a girl-friend. Or friends, period, for that matter, outside a few kids at the university.

"Do you happen to have her contact information?"

"Sure."

Laney handed Darcy her pad and watched as she wrote a name and number down. "That's her cell. Or was. I haven't talked to her since Devon's arrest, but I assume that's the number she still uses."

Laney accepted the pad back. "Thanks, Darcy."

"Don't mention it."

"GET READY for a night out. Dress casual. Pick you up at nine."

Laney returned to her office to find the note on her desk. It was unsigned, but she didn't have to wonder who it was from. No one else would dare be as confident to leave her such a message and expect her to honor it.

No one but Carter Southard.

Now she was at her penthouse, rating the contents of her walk-in closet.

She really needed this respite in the middle of the chaotic sea she was navigating at work. The police didn't have any clues about who might have vandalized her car or sent her the notes. Her defense options for Devon's trial were limited to questioning every piece of evidence the prosecution was going to present, hoping to chip away at it and create that all-important shadow of doubt. She'd spent the afternoon with the defense team, lining up charts and photos and following up with witnesses to make sure everything—at least from an organizational standpoint—would go smoothly. Junior attorneys Dave Matthews and Matt Johnson would be cocounsels, along with senior partner Harold Reasoner.

Normally, she would be spending the night going over her opening statement, editing it, reworking it. Sleep would be the last thing on her agenda, much less any thought of fun. But when she'd read the note, and remembered her night with Carter, she knew that a fresh perspective was exactly what she needed at this point.

At least that's what she told herself. If the thought of seeing Carter made her want to leave the real world behind for just a few precious hours, she wasn't admitting it.

She stood before her open closet door. Casual. He'd said to be casual. The word could mean anything. There were at least three categories of casual. There was the "clean out the garage" variety, where old jeans, T-shirt and tennis shoes were the name of the game. The "let's go out for pizza" casual. And "dressy casual."

Okay, she could rule out the first one. Even Carter wouldn't take her to clean out his garage at nine o'clock on a Friday night.

But he had said "a night out" which could mean comfortable shoes for a walk through the downtown district.

Oh, what was she worried about? He'd be there in five minutes. She could find out exactly where he planned to take her and decide if what she had on was too dressy or not.

She dumped the pile of discarded clothes onto the floor and then closed the closet doors. She hadn't tried on more than two outfits for a night out in a long time. Especially not for a casual one.

Then why did her stomach feel as if the bottom had been cut out of it? And why did every inch of her skin tingle as if Carter had just blown his hot breath against it?

The intercom rang.

"Mr. Southard would like you to meet him at the curb, Ms. Cartwright."

"Thanks, Roger."

Damn. So much for her plan to change clothes if need be. Looked like she was stuck with what she had on—a gauzy white skirt, short tan cowboy boots and a white, scoop-necked top. Just to be on the safe side, she grabbed a light tan jacket and hurried to meet him.

"Evening, Ms. Cartwright," the doorman said.

"Hello, Roger. Where…"

She spotted Carter leaning against his motorcycle by the curb. A shiver of awareness drifted over her at the sight of him. His booted feet were crossed at the ankles, and a crisp white T-shirt pulled tight over his wide chest. His arms were crossed in front of him, emphasizing the width of his triceps and calling attention to his USMC tattoo. He wore a brown leather vest over his T-shirt and a matching cowboy hat. Sunglasses blocked his expression as he watched her come through the door.

"Something tells me I might not be dressed appropriately," she said, twisting her lips wryly.

"You worry too much about the unimportant. You're dressed just fine."

She gestured toward the bike. "Not for riding that."

"Why not?"

A challenge. He was challenging her. She looked down at her skirt. Given the slightly translucent quality of the fabric, it fell in several layers to just below her knees. She'd never ridden on a bike before, let alone in a skirt. But her father liked to joke that she was born on the back of a horse, and she'd spent a great deal of time in the stables on her father's estate while growing up. Surely the two couldn't be all that different.

Carter threw his right leg over the seat and started the engine. The loud roar evened out to a strong purr as he patted the seat behind him.

Fine.

Laney bunched the front of her skirt up to the top of her thighs, acutely aware he was watching her every move, and then straddled the bike behind him, scooting up close and personal.

"Mmm, am I doing it right?" she whispered into his ear, finding something very appealing about sitting so close to him. He smelled of laundry detergent and limes.

He handed her a black helmet that came to just over her ears and strapped under her chin. "You're doing it just perfect, darlin'."

The Harley leaped forward. Laney grabbed him around the waist to keep from falling off. She caught his naughty grin in the rearview mirror and knew instantly that he'd done that on purpose. She scooted closer so that her crotch rested against the back of his jeans. His grin melted into a suggestive smile.

The engine humming beneath Laney was oddly relaxing. The open air around her was freeing. The man between her thighs was hot. The engine also helped drown out the sounds of other vehicles around them. In fact, the world seemed to fade away, leaving just her, Carter and the bike.

For a moment, she wished that he didn't have anything planned other than a nice, long ride out of town. She wanted to see what the summer sky looked like from the back of the bike when darkness began to fall and the stars dotted the night.

She flattened her hands against his waist and slid them around until they rested low on his hard abs. She felt his quick intake of breath and smiled, her cheek resting against his shoulder. The rich scent of leather and cotton teased her senses as she watched the city streets quickly give way to the suburbs and then the wide, open plains.

Mmm, yes. In that one instant she wanted for nothing.

Unfortunately, Carter apparently did have a destination in mind. The bike slowed and he pulled off the road. Laney reluctantly lifted her chin and found they were at a place they had passed a good twenty minutes ago.

"You could have kept going," she said into Carter's ear.

"And miss what I have in mind? Not a chance."

Laney climbed off the bike, immediately missing the vibration. Carter pushed the Harley up onto its stand and climbed off. He took his hat off, ran his fingers through his hair and grinned at her.

"You ready?"

"Ready for what?"

He nodded toward the honky-tonk next door.

She smiled back at him. "I was born ready."

MAGGIE'S BOOT-SCOOTIN' Saloon was not a place Ms. Laney Cartwright would have ever entered on her own steam. Still, even in her designer duds, and obviously out of her element, she was up for the challenge he'd presented her with.

Of course, if he was having trouble answering *why* he'd felt compelled to challenge her, well, that was between him and the dance floor.

Truth was, he'd been struggling with his fierce reaction to their lovemaking the other night. Despite his experience, he was sure that his memory of her satiny smooth skin, the sound of her soft sighs, the perfect sex had to be an illusion, something conjured up by a subconscious that had been searching for the same but had never found it. There was no way it was real. It couldn't be. Because stuff like that didn't exist. And even if it did, it never happened to him.

With his hand low on her back, he led Laney toward the long bar at the far end of the large saloon, watching her look around in fascination. The place was already packed to overflowing with some people seated and enjoying dinner from the limited menu of fried items, others jumping on the dance floor, blocking a clear view of the band that filled the large area with heart-pulsing country and western music.

"What'll you have?" the barmaid asked him. Her tight T-shirt had Maggie's written across it.

Carter looked at Laney.

She shrugged. "Order for me."

He placed a request for two bottles of beer and then leaned against the bar.

Laney sparkled like a polished diamond among the rough rocks around her. Carter didn't come to places like this much himself, but he'd been curious to see how Laney might react in unfamiliar territory.

Their beers were delivered and Carter paid for them, handing Laney hers. She thanked him and took a long sip, licking her lips in a way that made his groin tighten.

The song ended and the band slid into a slow ballad, the lights going low. The dance floor filled with couples.

Laney put her bottle on the bar. "So, cowboy, were you planning on asking me to dance? Or did we just come here to watch?"

9

LANEY'S HEAD was cloudy and she felt unsteady on her feet. But she'd only had a sip of beer, so she couldn't be drunk. At least not on beer. But as Carter skillfully led her around the dance floor in a boot-dragging two-step, his beer bottle hanging from his hooked index finger over her left shoulder, she was afraid that if she were given a Breathalyzer test, she'd be way over the legal limit for what any hot-blooded woman could take while in the arms of a hot man.

Oh, she knew how to dance. While she'd never been to a place like Maggie's, a good Texas girl didn't pass the age of seven without knowing how to two-step. But in the venues where she usually danced, the couples looked more as if they were doing a Viennese waltz, not what the people around her were doing.

What she and Carter were doing.

Every time he got the chance, he brushed the top of his hard thigh between her legs. The first time she'd gasped and nearly stumbled, the electricity joining her to him nearly knocking her off balance. The second time wasn't any better. But then she fell into the easy, naughty rhythm he set, doing a bit of tantalizing of her own by grazing the tips of her breasts against his chest just so, rubbing her nose against the line of his jaw like that, until they weren't so much two people but one.

Laney's eyelids drifted closed, and again she experienced that strange feeling that the world had fallen away, leaving just the small bit of earth they stood on. She surrendered to the beat of the music. To the feel of Carter against her. To the yearnings of her own heart.

"You keep moving against me like that, Ms. Cartwright, I'm not sure what I'll do," Carter whispered into her ear.

She shivered from boot to earring, thinking that whatever he had in mind, she'd welcome it wholeheartedly. "I could say the same of you, Mr. Southard."

They danced through this set and into the next, their beer forgotten as they gave themselves over to the music and their growing desire, bodies shimmying and shaking and brushing up against each other in a primitive rite as old as time.

The overhead lights were turned on and off and final call for alcohol made. Laney was genuinely surprised they'd spent the whole night there. It felt as if they'd just arrived.

"Let's get out of here," Carter said, grasping her hand and leading her toward the door.

Laney was only too happy to oblige.

TOO FAST...

The two words ran around and around Carter's mind

as he rode back toward the city, Laney wrapped around him from behind. Even though he couldn't look into her face, he had the distinct feeling that he was drowning in her big, blue eyes.

Christ, what was going on? He'd meant to have a simple fling. Sleep with her and move on. But with every moment that passed, he wanted to spend another day with her. Couldn't seem to shake her from his mind, couldn't stop his body from wanting hers.

He pulled off an exit ramp just short of the turnoff for the city. Laney shifted.

"Where are we going?"

He didn't answer her.

"Are you taking me to your place?"

Oh, hell no. The last place he would ever take her was to his place.

Then again, maybe it was exactly the place he should take her. But he wasn't ready for that. Not yet. Baring that much of his life made him feel sick to his stomach.

Instead, he pulled off into the parking lot of an old roadhouse bar. There were other bikes and beat-up pickup trucks in front. He'd never been to this particular bar before, but he'd spent his fair share of time in others just like it.

"What's this?" Laney asked as he got off the bike to stand next to her.

"I thought we might stop for a nightcap."

He didn't miss her frown, despite her attempt to cover it up. "I thought we had enough at the saloon."

He grinned and led her to the door. It opened, spitting out two guys staggering their way into the night. Carter caught it and motioned for her to enter. She did so. And the reservation he'd expected to see at the saloon came out clearly now.

The clientele here weren't dressed in their Sunday best. Most of them wore the same clothes they'd probably worked in that day, filling the interior of the establishment with the smell of unwashed bodies and beer. He even detected the stench of vomit, and the bleach-based cleaner the owner had probably used to try to cover it.

Three quarters of the bar's patrons were male and more than halfway toward their next hangover. Carter pulled out a stool for Laney at the long, battle-scarred bar and then sat next to her. The stocky bartender asked him what they wanted.

"Give us two shots of Wild Turkey with draft chasers."

When the bartender walked away, Laney leaned closer to him. "Don't all places stop serving liquor at the same time?"

Carter grinned at her. "They're supposed to."

"Couldn't he lose his license?"

"Sure. If anyone reported him." He nodded toward the clientele. Those who didn't have their chins resting against the top of their glasses were openly appreciating Laney's presence. "I think that's the last thing on any of these guys' minds."

The bartender served them and then slid over a bowl

of cheap peanuts sitting in front of another customer who paid him no mind. In the corner, the jukebox blared a Hank Williams classic that somehow held a different kind of meaning in a place like this. Rather than inspiring patrons to dance, it stirred them to order another drink.

"God," Laney said quietly, "I haven't been here five minutes and I'm already feeling sorry for myself."

Carter raised his shot glass and she did the same. "To real life."

She searched his face. "To a more upbeat song."

Laney shuddered as she swallowed the bourbon. He pushed the glass of beer toward her and she grasped it with both hands, taking a long pull from the foamy depths.

She coughed into her hand. "So…come here often?"

Carter dropped his head and grinned. "Not here. No. But to a place like this."

She squinted at him. Down the bar to his right sat a young couple, likely married. They'd both obviously drunk more than they should have and were beginning to argue. The man accused her of flirting with a guy at one of the two pool tables. She accused him of being more like a father than a husband, offering up her wrist as proof that he had no shackles on her.

Laney somehow managed to shut the argument out as she continued looking at him.

"Why?"

The simple word was enough to knock Carter back on his boot heels.

"Why not?" he said back.

The people here were more like him than the people who ran in her circles. The beer was cheap, the surroundings unassuming; the jukebox had a good selection of oldies, and the kitchen could even rustle up a bowl of chili or nachos or a burger for you if you didn't feel like going anywhere else to eat.

The wife of the arguing couple stormed off in the direction of the restrooms, staggering through the smattering of tables and their occupants toward the hall at the far end of the room.

Carter finished his beer and put in an order for another round, shots included.

He didn't miss Laney's frown. It was the first he'd seen from her. And although it was what he'd been angling for all night, now that he had it, he wanted to wipe it away and replace it with one of her beautiful smiles.

"Excuse me for a moment, won't you?" she asked.

He watched as she followed the path of the angry wife, stopping in front of the jukebox to feed a dollar into the machine and making a couple of selections before continuing on.

It didn't take a sober man to know that she didn't fit in here.

She didn't fit with him.

And the sooner they both woke up to that fact, the better.

LANEY CAREFULLY MANEUVERED her way around a suspicious puddle outside the men's room and continued down the dim hallway to the door to the ladies'. This had to be one of the most god-awful places she'd ever been to. If it were true that every face told a story, then the stories in this place spoke of hardship and loneliness. Not that she didn't know people who were struggling and lonely. She'd just never seen them look as bad.

She pushed open the door, only to find something blocking it.

She heard a string of curse words and then, "Can't you see the damn thing is occupied?"

A man's hand curved around the edge and opened the door a little wider. Laney caught an eyeful of the drunken wife sitting with her pants off on the single bathroom sink, the man her husband had accused her of flirting with filling the space between her thighs.

He grinned at Laney. "Maybe she wants to make this a threesome."

The woman lit into him the same way she had to her husband not two minutes ago.

"Excuse me," Laney said, quickly making her way back down the hall and through the bar, not stopping until she was standing outside, drawing in a lungful of air.

Carter joined her. "Everything all right?"

"I think I've had about enough of the real world that I can take just now." She tried for a smile but failed as someone nearby retched. "If it's all the same to you, I'd like to call it a night."

Within moments, she was on the back of Carter's bike. She held on to him tightly, but for different reasons than she had earlier. She remembered the file the JAG attorney had faxed over to her. The brief rendering of a man she didn't know. A man different from the Carter Southard she'd met. But he wasn't different, was he? He was the same man. He was just letting her see a different part of himself.

They arrived back at her place quicker than she would have thought possible. After her experience, she'd expected it to take hours to return to her familiar world. Instead, it was right outside her back door, so to speak. She had just chosen not to see it.

"Are you all right?" Carter asked.

She swallowed hard as she stared up at her apartment building. "Fine. I must have had a little too much to drink, is all."

They both knew that she hadn't, but thankfully he didn't push the issue.

"Well, then, I'd better get going."

Laney looked at him in surprise. It was then that she realized he'd done what he had on purpose. That just as she'd been angling for a reaction from him at Raphael's, he'd been trying to provoke one from her tonight.

And, to her horror, he'd succeeded.

"Oh, no," she said. "There's no way you're leaving this bad taste in my mouth." She reached up and pushed his hat back off his head, forcing him to catch it as she thrust her fingers into the soft depths of his hair. Then she kissed him hard. "You're not going anywhere but upstairs with me."

She took his keys from him and tossed them to the doorman as they went inside. "See to the bike for me, won't you, Roger?"

She ignored Roger's bewildered expression as she pulled Carter into the elevator and pressed the button for the penthouse.

10

LANEY KNELT on the mattress in front of Carter, who stood next to the bed. She'd stripped out of her clothes and now took her time taking off his. He'd barely said two words since they'd come in, his handsome face drawn into the long lines she'd seen on too many of the faces at the bar he'd taken her to.

How close was he to being one of those men? Outside of the Marines, what did he do? She'd never asked him.

And she wasn't about to now, either. She wanted, needed to speak to him in a way that didn't require words. Was compelled to communicate what she was feeling.

She reached up, smoothing her fingertips over the strong planes of his face, over his cheeks, up to his forehead. So handsome. She pushed his thick hair back over and over again and then pressed her mouth against his, kissing him lingeringly.

It was somehow important for him to know that while she'd been knocked off balance by the glimpse he'd given her into his life, she was able to take a step back and see what had passed between them in an objective light.

She dipped her tongue between his lips, tasting Wild Turkey and beer.

Objective? Who was she kidding? What was happening had nothing to do with objectivity. Because if she were thinking with her head, she'd admit that she and the hot Marine had virtually nothing in common outside their combustible desire for each other. And that to take things any further, to tempt fate and feed her fear that she was falling for him might very well be the dumbest thing she'd ever done.

Carter had been impassive to her advances, watching her through half-lidded eyes as she kissed him. But as she scooted closer to him on her knees, snaking her hands under his arms and around his waist, pressing her bare breasts against his chest, feeling his arousal against her lower belly, she knew that he wouldn't be able to resist her for long. Hoped he wouldn't.

He groaned low in his throat and cupped her face in his hands, deepening their kiss. Laney knew a relief so complete she nearly melted to the mattress in a puddle of need.

Carter nudged her back. Laney walked on her knees and he knelt on the bed in front of her, moving until they were in the middle. He kissed her fiercely, entangling his fingers in her hair, the side of his hand resting against her neck. Heat rushed over Laney, her heart beating an unsteady rhythm in her chest.

What was it about this one man that made her want to reach out to him? Was it merely the sex? But she knew that couldn't be the only reason. She was no amateur when it came to dating. She'd slept with men before. Had even experienced some fantastic orgasms. But all of them paled in comparison to the sensations Carter inspired in her. He seemed able to reach deeper, demanding something within her she hadn't known existed.

He was her opposite in so many ways.

Yet they fit as completely as a love letter in an envelope.

Carter slid his hands down her neck and over her shoulders, bringing her closer so that her breasts brushed against his chest. Laney's mouth dropped open and he kissed her upper lip and then her lower until she came back to him, the thrum of her pulse growing louder in her ears. He cupped her right breast, running the pad of his callused thumb over her nipple and then back again. Tendrils of red-hot heat unfurled across her stomach, pooling in the apex of her thighs.

He moved his hands around to her back, pressing his fingers into her flesh and then driving them down until he reached the crease of her bottom. He filled his palms with her, his fingertips dipping into her crevice from behind. Laney curved her arms under his and held tight to his shoulders, relishing the languid need gathering deep in her belly.

There was no need to rush. No urgency. Time didn't exist. She was aware only of the flow of blood through her veins and the hands of the man touching her.

Carter sat back on his heels and wrapped her legs around his hips, pulling her flush against his hard arousal. She wasn't sure when he'd sheathed himself, only knew that he had. And in one, slow stroke, he filled her to overflowing.

Laney gasped, feeling as if every molecule of air had been forced from her body, leaving nothing but trembling desire in its wake.

Carter grasped her bottom, pushing her up and then down his rock-hard length. Laney dropped her head back. He nuzzled her neck as his every stroke seemed to go deeper, and deeper still.

She'd felt chaotic the first time they'd had sex, but this time…now…a throbbing, consuming heat claimed her inside and out. It was as if she were burning alive. And she didn't want to put out the fire; she wanted to feed it.

She rubbed her hands down the muscular lines of his back again and again, the rasp of her nipples against the crisp hair on his chest fanning the flames further. She kissed him, her mouth bowing open as he thrust inside her, then she kissed him again, looking deep into his eyes, seeing in them the intensity of emotion crowding her own body.

She couldn't take it…every move emerged a sweet torture. Laney crossed her ankles behind his back and braced her hands against his shoulders, allowing him to set the rhythm, giving herself over to him to do what he would.

Yes…no…the words swirled in her head. Yes, yes, please…no, no, don't ever stop…

One long stroke that made her catch her breath, then

another, and Laney climaxed, exploding into a million shiny pieces, somehow managing to hold on as Carter came, as well, his groan filling her ear along with his hot breath.

THE FOLLOWING AFTERNOON, Carter sat on his back porch with a bottle of lemonade, Blue lying on the ground at his feet, panting. This morning he'd woken up next to Laney, thinking himself in a dream. It couldn't possibly be real. Everything was white, soft, beautiful. Especially the woman lying asleep next to him, her milky hip bare where the sheet had fallen partially off during the night.

He'd hated to wake her. Hated to wake up himself. But a mechanism from the battlefield kicked in—a sort of survival technique that would protect him against an oncoming attack.

The problem was that when he stroked her satiny skin, and her blue eyes blinked open and she smiled, the dream had become even more exquisite instead of dissipating.

"Good morning," she said, stretching her arm across his waist and kissing his chest, her white-blond hair an angelic tangle of curls around her face.

He'd remembered she'd said something about meeting her father for brunch, so he'd reminded her then. Anything to stop the ache that had begun to grow deep in his gut the night before. To stop himself from giving in to the need to make love to her again.

Laney had seemed to tune in to his diversionary

tactic, but hadn't said anything. Instead, she'd made them both eggs for breakfast. And he found out that she had more than a few things on her mind.

"By the way, I heard from your JAG attorney," she'd said casually.

He'd squinted at her. She must have gotten the information yesterday at the latest, and was just now saying something.

"I'm sorry," she'd said, putting down her toast and brushing her hands together. "I meant to tell you last night, but I completely forgot. Forgive me?"

The way she'd smiled at him with her neat, white teeth made him think he'd forgive anything.

And that was an even bigger problem.

It wasn't so long ago that he'd sworn he wouldn't allow another woman to hurt him. Since JoEllen Atchison had accused him of attempted rape. He hadn't been allowed to defend himself and had wound up in jail without a prayer of getting out.

Until an angel in the shape of Laney Cartwright sprung him.

Now…

Well, now he was afraid he was coming to care for Laney in a way that transcended anything he'd experienced. No matter what the differences between them, perhaps even because of them.

There was so much she didn't know about the world. So much she'd been protected from.

He remembered her reaction to having her tires

slashed. And her pale face when she'd rushed out of the bar last night.

Carter cringed. He'd been trying to make a point. A point that was moot considering where they were now.

And where were they?

Old Blue looked up at him and rolled his long tongue along his moist chops, giving a small whine. If he didn't know better, Carter would say that hound had heard his question and was saying, "Beats the hell out of me, buster."

Time. He needed to give himself some time to think about what was happening between him and the lady lawyer. Problem was, time was his greatest enemy. He had too damn much of it on his hands now that the Marines had kicked his no-good ass out.

"I understand you've been given a list of criteria you need to meet before the Corps will consider your reinstatement?" Laney had asked him at breakfast.

He'd nodded and avoided meeting her gaze.

Oh, he'd been given a list, all right. And at the top was going to that damn group meeting. Something he had no intention of doing.

Laney had laid her hand with its short, red nails against his arm. "You have to do it, Carter," she'd said as if he'd mouthed his thoughts aloud. "Unless…"

"Unless what?"

She'd removed her hand and sat up a little straighter. "Unless you decide you'd rather take your life in another direction."

Another direction? There was nothing else he'd ever

considered doing outside the military. His father had been a Marine, and he was a Marine. It was as complicated and as a simple as that.

And if the Corps refused to reinstate him?

Suddenly Carter felt sick.

"Come on, Blue," he said to the dog. "Let's go for a walk."

The old hound lifted his head but didn't get up.

"Fine. I'll go for a walk by myself, then."

He had to do something, anything, to keep himself from calling Laney.

Time. He needed time.

If only there wasn't so damn much of it to fill.

11

AGAIN, TWO DAYS HAD PASSED and there had been no contact from Carter. And no matter what Laney did, she couldn't help worrying that she might never see him again.

It was late Monday morning. There was one week left before the MacGregor trial began. And she couldn't seem to keep her mind on anything other than the phone—wishing it would ring, and when it did, hoping it was Carter.

"Laney?" her associate Dave Matthews asked across the conference table that was serving as the war room for the trial.

"Hmm?" She glanced away from the telephone extension in the room. "Oh, yes. I think we should go with the new time line. It's much clearer than the old one."

And with that, Matt and Dave began tossing other ideas around, leaving her to sit back in her chair and review her notes. Written in large letters was "Meet Tiffany at 12:30, coffee shop." Laney checked her watch. It was nearly noon already.

She rubbed her forehead, marveling at how slowly

time seemed to go by minute by minute, yet zoomed by in batches when she wasn't paying attention.

"Why don't we break for lunch?" she said. "We can meet back here, say, in an hour and a half?"

She hadn't told either one of her colleagues about the existence of a girlfriend in the case. She wanted to feel things out first. See if Devon had still been seeing Tiffany when he was arrested before his lawyers all skipped down an avenue that might be a dead end.

She'd called the number Devon's sister had given her and requested the meeting.

"Yeah, I know who you are," Tiffany had said when she'd introduced herself over the phone. "You're that lawyer bitch representing Devon."

"Laney will do, thank you," she'd said in response, trying to remember the last time she'd been called the B word. At least two years, she believed. After she'd successfully defended her first client and the prosecutor had glared at her smile. She hadn't realized he'd expected her to lose until that moment.

Anyway, Tiffany had agreed to meet her today, first suggesting a park in Irving, then grudgingly settling on the coffee shop in the west end.

Laney drove there, parked at the curb, then went inside. She was ten minutes early. And, so it seemed, was Tiffany.

Her hair color could be anything under the black dye job, and her pale skin was peppered with several piercings. She was wearing a short, short black skirt and a too-small tank top that left her stomach bare and high-lighted the additional navel piercing.

This was Devon's girlfriend? She would never have picked her out of a lineup of possibilities.

"It's the lawyer bitch."

Laney winced. It was one thing being called that over the phone. Another to your face. "Laney will do fine," she repeated, searching for any sign of human warmth in the young woman in front of her. She saw none. Tiffany's dark eyes were hard and inscrutable. Spite oozed from her every pore. And she looked as though she would like nothing better than to get Laney's tan suit dirty.

"Does D know you're here?" Tiffany asked.

Laney refused to let her lead the conversation. "I think you should be more curious about what I'm doing here."

"And that is?"

"I want you to tell me what you know about that night."

Tiffany laughed, revealing that the piercings weren't limited to her skin. Her tongue was spiked with what looked like a barbell. Laney shuddered.

"Well, then," Laney said, "maybe you'd like to tell me who would want to set Devon up."

Tiffany's lips firmed. "What makes you think he was set up?"

"Are you telling me he did it?"

"I'm not saying nothing."

"Why did you agree to meet me here then?"

"You tell me."

Laney was losing patience, fast. What was Devon doing going out with a girl like Tiffany? And had his sister Darcy met her? Or had she only been in contact via cell phone?

It didn't make any sense.

"Look, Tiffany, I'm not here to play cat and mouse. I was hoping you might be able to help me in Devon's defense."

"Ain't no way in hell I'm going anywhere near a courthouse again."

Again.

Laney didn't miss the word.

She squinted at the young woman whose future looked about as bright as her hair color.

"I'm not suggesting you do," she said. "But I would like to ask you a few questions. Like how long you and Devon have been dating. Are you still seeing each other now? Where were you on the night of the robbery—"

Tiffany held up a black-nailed hand. "Forget you. I'm out of here."

The girl started to walk away and Laney did something completely out of character. She grabbed her arm to stop her.

Tiffany looked as if she'd like nothing more than to hit her.

Laney was pretty sure her expression displayed the same thing.

"I'm going to ask you one last time, Tiffany. Who would want to set Devon up?"

The girl set her jaw.

"Or should I be asking why *you* would want to set him up?"

IT APPEARED more and more likely that Carter wouldn't be invited back into the Marines any time soon.

Which meant he would have to start searching out an alternative lifestyle.

The thought would have seemed unimaginable even three months ago. But now Carter sat at his kitchen table with a pad and pen, ready to accept that his military career had reached its end.

He stared at the blank page and then scratched his head. A thousand ideas presented themselves to him, each immediately rejected. Truth was, he'd never considered a life outside the military. Men in every generation of Southards had served, with his father it being a career. It was understood that he would follow in his father's footsteps, straight into killed-in-action if need be.

But what did he do when that option was taken away from him?

He pulled the manila envelope sitting on the corner of the table closer to him, opening the flap and sliding out the documentation there. The small packet represented the whole of his life. From his birth certificate and passport to his Special Ops certification and his suspension papers. He found the paper that he wanted and smoothed it out on top of the pad. It was a list of steps he was required to take before being reconsidered for reinstatement.

It was surprising to him that he was contemplating not taking those steps. But something in him had changed when he'd been wrongfully arrested. Actually, he suspected the change had begun long before that, dating back to the incident that had ended with his suspension in the first place.

He rubbed his face and then looked at his hands. They bore cuts and oil stains that he hadn't been able to scrub out after working on his property clearing dry brush that could easily catch fire in the summer heat, then doing some maintenance on his bike in the garage. He'd always been a good mechanic. He'd even worked a stint at a full-service garage when he was sixteen, up the road at Old Man Johnson's place. His father had been pleased with him when he'd come home with his first paycheck.

"A man should always be self-sufficient," he'd said, and then given him an awkward pat on the back.

Carter would like to say that their relationship was peppered with such exchanges, but the elder Southard had never been comfortable with displays of affection. And Carter seemed to have inherited the gene.

The long stretches of time when the elder Southard was shipped out on assignment and father and son hadn't seen each other were at least partly to blame. But not totally. Because during those stints, neighbors and the families of his father's army buddies had stepped in to take care of him until he was old enough to look after himself, so Carter had been exposed to lifestyles different from his own.

Still, he'd always felt like an outsider.

He'd been on his own since he'd landed that first job at Johnson's garage. The old guy had finally kicked the bucket sometime last year. He'd never been married and was childless, so the garage sat abandoned.

It was funny how quickly the land could reclaim a structure. Weeds grew up through cracks in the asphalt of the parking lot, and ivy was growing over the side of the building and its three bay doors. Even the blue lettering announcing Johnson's Car Garage seemed to have faded quickly in the strong Texan sun.

Every time Carter passed the property and the For Sale sign tacked to the door, he remembered the summer he'd worked there. But he'd certainly never thought of working there again.

Now, he pushed the paper outlining Marine requirements aside and picked up the pen, writing "Reopen Johnson's place" across the first page of the pad and underlining it several times. His skills might be a little rusty, but he could always hire somebody who could pick up the slack until he felt he was up to snuff.

An odd gust of wind blew in through the back door, bringing the afternoon heat with it. The paper he'd pushed aside shifted to rest on top of the pad, the words seeming to stare up at him.

He folded it and stuffed it back into the envelope, trying not to think about how one Ms. Laney Cartwright would react to seeing him wearing a work jumpsuit, covered in oil.

He winced. It was just as well that they were ending things the way they were.

SOMETIMES LANEY'S FATHER told her that he didn't know why she drove herself the way she did. Lord knew she didn't have to. Had she chosen to live a life of leisure, she certainly had the resources with which to do so. In fact, several of her girlfriends from high school and college led perfectly simple lives defined by the many social events they attended rather than a time clock. Those who weren't already married with kids, that is.

Oh, to only have a time clock.

She stared at her watch. Past nine. She'd been working for fourteen hours straight. And her body was letting her know it. She had a crick in her neck and her lower back nearly gave out as she finally rose from the exhibit and file-covered conference table.

She stepped out of the room and looked around the deserted hall. She'd sent Dave and Matt home a couple of hours ago, but had wanted to finish up a few things herself while they were still fresh in her mind. She blinked and flicked off the lights before going to her office. She glanced at her messages; replies could wait until tomorrow. Then she gathered her purse and briefcase and headed for the elevator. The lawyers had ordered in dinner but she'd eaten very little of it, so her stomach felt empty and odd. Still, she couldn't think of a thing she'd like to eat. An omelet, maybe, at home. Something light and packed full of protein this late.

Within fifteen minutes, she was greeting Roger the doorman and getting into the elevator to take her up to the penthouse. Her head felt good and fried. Maybe she would just take a shower and call it a night.

It took her a few moments to find the right key on her chain and finally she was opening the door to a place that usually brought her joy but now only gaped large and empty. White on white on white, the décor loomed cold and unwelcoming instead of plush and pristine as she'd intended. Not even switching on lights and having light from the setting sun streaming through the sheers at the balcony doors did much to change how she felt.

She was just tired, that's all, she told herself. She loved this apartment. It reflected every part of her. Was exactly the way she wanted it.

Why, then, did she feel ill at ease?

She put her purse and briefcase down on the foyer table and kicked off her shoes, shrugging out of her suit jacket as she padded across the thick white carpeting toward her bedroom and the master bath.

Then it became clear why she felt uncomfortable in her own home: someone had been there.

12

"Come, Carter, I need you…"

Laney's plea had him springing into action. Where it usually took a half hour to reach downtown, he made it in half that time, displaying his impatience to the doorman, who appeared intent on protecting Laney himself.

Now he stood off to one side in her penthouse apartment, a silent dark shadow against the brightness of the place, watching as the police finished making notes.

The door finally closed behind them and Laney launched herself into his arms.

"Thank God, you're here," she whispered. "I couldn't think of anyone else to call. My father's away on business and…"

He wanted to tell her that no explanation was needed but couldn't form words as he folded her easily against his tense frame.

"What happened?" he asked, looking around, trying to discern what had compelled her to call him for help.

"There was a break-in…my bedroom…"

He gently set her aside and walked to the doorway of the room in question. Swatches of color littered the top of the made bed and the floor. He walked inside and lifted what looked like a pair of panties. Only they'd been slashed in two so they appeared to be nothing more than squares of red silk.

"Every undergarment, slip, stocking and nightgown I own," Laney said from behind him.

"Christ."

He stood for a long moment, staring at the carnage.

"And there was another note."

He turned to face her.

Her usually flawless white skin was ashy as she looked away.

"What did it say, Laney?" Carter swore he could feel every drop of his blood as it rushed through his veins.

Her blue eyes looked up to meet his gaze. "Strike Three, You're Out."

He stood silently for a few moments before moving.

"What are you doing?" she asked.

Carter felt he had to do something, anything to expel the anger filling him. He was snatching the scraps of silky material up one by one from her bed and the floor and dropping them into a nearby wastebasket.

"How in the hell did they get in here?" He thought of Roger the doorman and had half a mind to go down and punish him for the crime.

"The best that Don, the day doorman, can figure is that the intruder must have gained access through the garage when one of the residents drove in. It would be simple enough to leave the same way once they were done."

"And the door to your apartment?"

"The police say there are scratches consistent with those made by a lock-picking kit."

Carter didn't stop until every splash of color in the white bedroom was gone. Then he picked up the wastebasket and marched through the apartment to the kitchen, where he found a garbage bag, dumping the contents inside. He tied the bag off and placed it outside in the hall, giving the door's locking mechanism a good look before closing it again.

Laney stood rubbing her hands over her arms. She seemed tired and scared, yet somehow she still managed to smile.

"The police say they're just trying to scare me." She laughed without humor. "Yeah, well, I figure they're doing a pretty good job."

"Do they have any leads on the first two notes?"

She shook her head. "No. The detective in charge says he's arranged for patrol cars to come by every half hour or so to check on things, but until he has evidence of a more serious crime, there's not much else he can do."

"A more serious crime? Like when you're attacked?"

He didn't think it was possible, but she grew even paler. Damn.

She smiled again. "I know there's probably little chance that anything more will happen tonight, but I was hoping that you might stay with me until morning?"

Carter was moved by her soft question.

She laughed again. "Oh, well. So much for me trying to charm you with my independent-woman-of-means role."

Carter stepped across the room and tucked her to his chest again, relieved when she melted against him.

"You're stronger than any person I've ever met, Laney." He smoothed her hair back from her face and stared into her doubtful yet hopeful eyes. "Let's just say that whoever's doing this better hope they never meet you in a dark alley."

She shuddered. "Please don't mention alleys and dark places right now."

Carter silently cursed himself again, moving his hands down her long back, trying to ignore his immediate and powerful response to her nearness.

"Have you eaten yet?" he asked.

She rubbed her nose against the sleeve of his T-shirt. "You know, for a macho Marine, you're awfully concerned with feeding me."

"That's because I like my women strong."

She laughed, a more generous sound now.

He gripped her arms and held her away from him before his growing erection began to dictate his actions.

"Why don't you go change while I whip us up something to eat?"

There was a curious light in her eyes as she stared at him for a long moment. "Yes. Okay."

She turned to walk back to her bedroom, hesitating as she looked around, as if expecting to find her shredded undergarments still littering the place. Then she disappeared into the master bath.

Carter drew in a deep breath and let it out again.

So much for keeping his distance from her.

LANEY WOKE with a start around 4:00 a.m. She sprang upright in bed, her breathing filling her quiet, empty bedroom. In her dream, she'd been asleep in the same bed while a man in a black mask shredded her lingerie on top of her. Then, running out of material, had stood eyeing her.

Her hand immediately went to the other side of the bed. Empty.

To her relief, Carter had agreed to stay the night. He'd fed her the best omelet she'd ever had, and then tucked her into bed. If she was disappointed that he hadn't made any physical advances, she wasn't going to admit it. But she had been glad when he'd lain on top of the blankets and spooned with her, his front against her back, until she fell asleep.

But where was he now?

She stripped off the covers and moved her legs to hang over the side of the mattress, listening. There was nothing but the quiet hiss of the air-conditioning coming in from the overhead vent.

She started when she heard someone speak.

Carter?

Who would he be talking to at 4:00 a.m.?

She grabbed her robe and walked down the hall into the living room. There she found him, sprawled across her oversized sofa, one leg bent at the knee, his left arm crossed over his eyes. He was asleep.

Laney pulled her robe closer around her. What was he doing in here? Why had he left the bed and come to sleep on the couch? She swallowed hard, hurt more than she would have thought possible.

She'd hoped that his coming here so quickly last night meant that he still wanted her. That they still had something that could be worked out.

But watching him sleep alone on her couch, which looked small when it was large, made her feel oddly lonely.

He muttered in his sleep again and Laney jumped. Her nerves must still be on edge from last night, she reasoned. She leaned closer, trying to figure out what Carter was saying in short, vehement spurts.

"IED! Move!"

There was nothing unclear about that outburst.

Laney's heart pumped thickly in her chest as she connected his nightmare with the items she'd read in the psych report from his JAG attorney.

He was always so good with her. Together. Alert and clear. When she'd originally received his case material, she remembered thinking that it couldn't possibly be true. There was no indication that Carter suffered any residual effects from his service in Iraq and then Afghanistan.

Of course, she'd never had any personal contact with someone diagnosed with PTSD before, either.

"Carter?" she whispered, reaching out a hand to wake him.

He shouted something incoherent again, and she noted the sweat that dotted his upper lip and forehead.

"Carter?" she said a little louder.

He jackknifed into a sitting position, grabbing her wrist in his left hand while his right produced a gun she hadn't known he carried.

THE WAR ZONE slowly faded away into the shadows of Laney's apartment. Carter sucked in deep breaths, staring at where she stood in front of him, hands over her heart as if to protect it. From the gun he held. From him.

He let rip a long stream of curses as he realized he was holding his 9 mm on her. He laid the gun on the sofa and then dropped his head into his hands, gathering his wits about him.

He was there to protect Laney.

He had nearly been the one to harm her.

"I'm sorry," she said haltingly. "You were having a nightmare and I…"

He looked up at her abruptly. Was she really apologizing to him?

At that moment, his entire life was a nightmare.

"What are you doing with a gun?" she whispered.

He went to great lengths to disguise its presence, but he took his 9 mm with him everywhere. If not on his person, then in the seat compartment of his Harley. Always careful when he was carrying that she wouldn't accidentally bump it.

"What were you dreaming about?"

Carter got up quickly, grabbing the gun as an after-thought. "I've got to get out of here."

He put his boots on while leaning against the front door, trying not to notice the way Laney looked both sexy and vulnerable as she watched him.

He stood up and slid the gun into the back waist of his jeans. "You should be fine now. I'll make sure Roger knows you're alone."

She nodded, but didn't say anything.

He curled his fingers around the doorknob, then let it go, moving to stand in front of her. He thread his fingers through her tousled, short blond curls and kissed her deeply. Something, anything, to rid her beautiful face of the expression of fear and concern that he'd put there.

Then he walked out the door, not leaving until he heard her lock it after him.

13

A FEW HOURS LATER, Laney woke to an odd sound in the room. It wasn't possible someone else had broken in again so soon. Was it Carter? Had he come back? She wouldn't question how he had gotten in. If career Marine Carter wanted to get into a place, he'd get in, no questions asked. In fact, she wouldn't put it past him to force Roger to give him access to the building's master key.

There it was. The sound again. Almost like…

Panting.

She scooted across the bed and peered over the side. Stretched out on her white carpeting was the ugliest dog she'd ever seen. Her brows rose as the old hound raised red, droopy eyes to stare up at her and then licked his sagging chops, causing a line of slobber to drop onto her slippers.

Oh, yuck.

She spotted a note tucked under his plain brown leather collar. She carefully reached a hand out and took it.

This is Blue. I've left him to protect you. Just make sure he's taken outside to see to his business

at least three times, keep his food and water bowls
full and he won't be any trouble at all to you. But
a stranger would need to take care.
Carter

Laney smiled. He'd brought his dog over.

She sat up and Blue got up, too. They stayed like that
for a long moment, just looking at each other.

"Hi, Blue," she said, slowly extending her hand palm
down so he could get a sniff. "I'm Laney."

His wet nose nudged against her hand as if trying to
turn it over and he barked once, a loud, soulful sound.

Laney jumped. "My, whoever named you got it right,
didn't they?" She scratched one of his long ears. "I feel
like singing the blues myself, sometimes."

She carefully rose to her feet, deciding to leave her
drool-soaked slippers behind, and checked that Carter
had put two bowls in the corner of her kitchen, one containing water, the other dog food. Inside the pantry, she
found a mammoth bag of kibble. She closed the door
and leaned against it, watching as the old dog sauntered
over to his water bowl and slurped up a good portion,
getting even more on the tile around it.

Whatever Carter's sins, she suspected a heart of gold
beat in his wide chest. She'd spotted it when she first
laid eyes on him in that San Antonio jail. And despite
the frightening middle-of-the-night encounter, she knew
it for sure now.

Who else could love a butt-ugly hound like this one?

Blue gave a couple of short barks, as if reading her thoughts.

Laney crouched down to pet him heartily, murmuring her apologies. She smiled, not only because of Blue's welcoming response but because his presence meant that she would be seeing Carter.

"THAT BACKGROUND CHECK on Tiffany Mullins just came in," Violet said from the doorway of the war room sometime later.

Laney was bent over an enlarged photograph of the masked robber with Dave Matthews, diagramming differences between an unknown gunman and Devon MacGregor. As she rose, her lower back let her know it wasn't happy. She pressed one hand against it and reached to take the report from Violet with her other.

"Thanks, Vi."

It had been hours since she'd showered and left her penthouse apartment to Blue, with instructions to the daytime doorman to arrange to have the old hound walked. She'd been hoping that Carter would call, or otherwise indicate when she might see him again, but it hadn't happened yet and it was well into midafternoon.

"What is it?" Dave asked.

Laney read the report once, then went back to the beginning to reread it. Out of curiosity, she'd asked Violet to run the background check through the private investigation firm the lawyers retained. While Laney had expected to find a few odd misdemeanors, what she was looking at far surpassed expectations.

"Seems Devon's girlfriend has a rap sheet as long as my desk," she said, looking at him. "And included in it is an arrest for armed robbery of a convenience store."

THE LAST THING Laney imagined finding when she returned home was Carter fixing dinner in her kitchen. Nothing special, he said. Just a couple of steaks and a salad. Since she'd never had anyone cook dinner for her, it might as well have been a holiday feast.

It was after seven and she was beyond tired. Yet somehow seeing Carter salting slabs of steak and washing greens made her feel loads better. She patted the old hound that lay next to the counter stools and leaned in to kiss Carter on the cheek.

He chuckled. "Somehow I suddenly feel like the little lady of the house."

While his usual humor was injected into the remark, so was a bit of uneasiness—similar to Laney's own surprise at her casual greeting. She'd meant the kiss as a thank-you, but somehow it seemed to reveal much more.

Or maybe she was reading more into it than there was. Sometimes that happened after a long day of thinking too much.

She slowly sat down on one of the stools and slipped her heels off, rubbing her left arch absently. She decided the correct response was her first one: to keep things light. "Ah, I figured you for the traditional type. Keeping women barefoot and pregnant after they get married."

"Oh?" He dried the greens with paper towels and she stopped herself from telling him about the salad spin drier stocked under the sink. It was much more fun watching him do it this way. Large, strong hands delicately patting moisture from the delicate greens provided an interesting counterpoint to her workday.

"Is that why I'm already married with two point two kids, then?" he asked.

She smiled, glad that he was taking her lead and keeping things light. She'd had enough of heavy for now. "Touché."

"And what about you?" He left the leaves to dry and came around the counter to sit next to her. He touched her knee. Laney jumped and then frowned, guessing she was still mentally at work. Had anyone there touched her that way, she'd have threatened a lawsuit.

"Whoa, easy," he said quietly.

She took a deep breath and relaxed, enjoying the way he smoothed his fingers down over her calf. He nudged her hand away and gripped her ankle, moving her foot until it sat on the stool between his jean-clad legs. Then his long fingers began properly massaging her toes.

"Mmm, that feels good." And it did. Decadently good. Not only was he skillfully chasing away her weariness, he created tiny sparks of awareness that raced up the back of her leg, making her want to draw a road map for him to follow under her skirt.

"So? Are you going to answer my question?" he asked.

Laney considered him from beneath lowered lids. "What question?" His attention moved from her toes to the length of her foot and back again. Laney's panties dampened. "Oh, right. Why don't I have a wife who's barefoot and pregnant with two point two children…"

He ran the tip of his index finger along her arch, tickling her.

"All right, all right, uncle," she said.

He exchanged one foot for the other while Blue watched their activities from his spot on the floor, his panting periodically broken when he licked his moist chops.

"I don't know," Laney said. "I guess I've been so consumed with my career that I've never really thought about the rest of it. Not like my friends. They're incessantly talking about marriage and their biological clocks and life plans…"

She drifted off, wondering if he would consider giving her a full-body massage.

"I can understand that," Carter said quietly.

"What? Ticking biological clocks?"

"No. Being consumed by your career."

Laney met his gaze, seeing the sober shadow in his eyes. She slowly removed her foot from his hands, remembering last night.

There were few things that could have compelled her to call a halt to one of the best foot massages she'd ever had, but the memory of having a gun pulled on her was definitely one of them.

She instantly missed his hands on her, but had to go through the door he'd just opened.

"Are you armed now?" she asked quietly.

Carter stared at her for a long moment, likely following her line of thought. She couldn't read his emotions. Was that something they taught in the military? How to fashion the perfect poker face? If so, she guessed Carter had passed that test with flying colors.

He got up and went back into the prep area across the counter to wash his hands. "No," he said in answer to her question.

Laney didn't know if she was relieved or disappointed. While having the firearm pointed at her had been terrifying, the fact that he was packing and wasn't afraid to use it appealed to her on a primal level.

She hadn't felt threatened. She'd been surprised. And a little scared. More for him and what he must have been dreaming than any real concern for her own well-being.

Still, while she'd been around guns for most of her life—her father was a collector and an avid gun fan— and she knew how to shoot one, she didn't own one. Something her father had suggested she might like to consider now that her personal space had been violated.

Laney got up, patted Blue, who lifted his head into the gesture, and then nudged Carter aside so she could wash up herself.

"Let me get that," she said when he reached for the greens.

They worked in companionable silence for a few moments, Laney ripping the greens and cutting tomatoes and onions, Carter testing the stovetop grill on the industrial-size stainless steel oven that she rarely used because cooking for one was both not much fun and inconvenient.

"Have you had a chance to go over the JAG report yet?" she asked as casually as if she'd just requested him to pass the salt.

She suspected he might not have heard her over the sizzle of the steaks and considered repeating her question. But when he turned, she knew he had not only heard, he was having a hard time responding.

"Their requirements don't look all that complicated," she said, tossing the salad with the light dressing of olive oil, red wine vinegar and Dijon mustard she'd mixed. She put the bowl on the counter between two place mats.

"That's because they're not being asked of you."

She took out a bottle of rosé from the refrigerator and opened it, conceding the point. She had no idea how it felt to be in his position. Her superiors couldn't suspend her or bring her up on a court martial.

Still, avoidance had never been a tactic she'd employed when facing any problem, much less one as big as the problem staring Carter straight in the face.

"Beer?" she asked.

"Thanks."

She took out a bottle from the fridge, popped the top and handed it to him. His fingers folded over hers and remained for a heartbeat before he released them. She couldn't help thinking the gesture was a silent plea for her to drop the subject.

She poured herself a glass of wine, surprised to find her hand trembling ever so slightly because she knew she couldn't retreat and pretend the problem didn't exist.

"You know, the papers your attorney sent over didn't give an exact reason why you were sent up for suspension."

She watched the back of Carter's shoulders stiffen as he tended the steaks. "The Corps prefers to keep everything in-house."

Laney shivered as she took the loaf of French bread he'd brought out of its paper bag and cut a few slices.

"Is the incident what you were dreaming about last night when…"

She wondered if there was another way to say, "When you pulled the gun on me?"

"Can you get me the plates from the microwave?" he asked instead of responding.

There were plates in the microwave? She popped open the door and saw two plain stoneware plates. She touched one, felt it was hot and got a towel to protect her hands as she took the plates out. He'd thought of everything. A man who looked after every detail. She'd known that was the case when it came to their time in the bedroom.

Then why was it so difficult for him to honor the Corps requirements for reinstatement?

Carter didn't blink as he held the plates without protection, placing a steak on top of each and then putting them on the place mats at the counter.

"Do you want to talk or eat?" he asked with a raised brow as he switched off the grill and turned to face her.

"We can do both."

He smiled, but somehow it didn't reach his beautiful eyes. "I think your friends would be shocked to see you talk with your mouth full."

"Well, good thing they're not here, then, isn't it?"

At the smell of the steaks, Blue invaded the kitchen. Carter put a couple of cubes of meat he must have reserved for the old hound into his food bowl.

Laney rounded the counter and sat down, waiting until Carter sat next to her before filling a small bowl with salad and handing it to him, then another for herself.

"So…" she prompted.

He chewed on a piece of steak for a moment. "You're not going to let me enjoy this prime piece of beef, are you?"

"That depends."

"On what?"

"On whether you stop the smart-ass diversionary tactics and start talking to me like I know the worth of a half dollar."

The corners of his eyes crinkled as he continued to eat. "And how much is that?"

Laney stared at him as she put a bite into her mouth. The beef melted against her tongue. "Oh my god. That's got to rate among the best steaks I've ever tasted," she said, cutting another piece.

"So can we eat now?"

She laughed. "Yes. But just so you know, I plan on returning to this conversation as soon as we finish."

"We'll see about that."

She nodded, swallowed another bite, and then reached for her wineglass. "Yes, we will."

14

SHOULD I STAY or should I go?

What was it about this one woman that knocked him off-kilter? Compelled him to do one thing when he should be doing another?

Carter lay in her bed sometime later, out of breath, his skin coated in sweat, curving Laney's soft body against his side. God, he couldn't seem to get enough of her. The instant he thought that this was it, this was the mark they could never possibly improve upon, he'd reach yet another level with the busty blonde, making him wonder what in the hell he'd been doing wrong all these years. Because this, what they shared, was what those corny romance novels were packed with. Sexy women, bare-chested men, red-hot passion. Like the book open on Laney's nightstand.

Maybe the romance novel had something to do with it.

He reached for the book with the red cover and the word Blaze stamped across it and stared at the picture of a half-naked man.

"You read this stuff?"

Laney shifted her head where it rested against his

chest, her curls teasing his left nipple. He took in her smile as she said, "Mmm-hmm. You may want to give them a try. They might give you a new idea or two."

Carter flipped the book open to the part where she'd left off. "And here I thought I was doing pretty good without any help."

She laughed low in her throat. "Trust me, you're doing just fine in that department."

He read the steamy passage in the book, his brows lifting higher at every other sentence.

"Holy shit," he said.

Laney took the book from him. "Enough reading. What's say we get back to real-time action?"

"More?"

She straddled him, her round, milky breasts bouncing as she found her spot and reached for the box of condoms on the table next to the novel. "Oh, much, much more, I think."

Carter grasped her lush hips, stretching his neck to contain his groan as she slid over his hard, sheathed length. "Remind me to buy you a box of those books, will you?"

She leaned in and kissed him lingeringly. "What are you going to do when you see my supply of other playground toys?"

Carter met her gaze. The woman was going to be the end of him. She truly was.

"WHAT MADE YOU want to be a Marine?"

Carter's eyes drifted open an hour later. He lay on

his stomach across the bed, about ready to drop off to sleep. Had Laney just asked the question she had? How could she possibly hold a thought in her head after their sack sessions?

The digital clock on the bedside table read after midnight. They'd been going at it since nine. And he was exhausted. Surely she had to be, too?

He shifted his head to look at her. She lay on her back on the other side of him, rubbing the arch of her foot absently against his calf. She stared at the ceiling, but her attention wasn't on the plaster there.

"Uh-oh. Is this the part where you try to continue our predinner conversation?" he asked.

She turned her head to smile at him. "You're quick."

"Not as quick as I'd like. If I had my choice, you would have completely forgotten about the topic."

"Ah, so that was your intention all along."

"Yes, and apparently I failed the mission."

She laughed quietly. "We were talking about why you became a Marine."

"Actually, you were talking about it. I was thinking about contributing." Carter rolled onto his back and drew in a deep breath.

Her hand touched his upper thigh. He could try distracting her with sex again. But, good Lord, he didn't think he had it in him.

Easier to respond to her blasted questions.

"I never wanted to be anything else," he answered honestly enough, staring at the ceiling himself.

She was quiet, but he could feel her gaze on his profile, the soft, idle stroking of her fingers against his thigh.

He should have known that wouldn't be enough. But he had hoped.

"Why?"

The question hated by men the world over. Right after, "What are you thinking?"

Carter swallowed hard, reminding himself that he did have a choice. But given his wrecked physical state, his options were limited. He couldn't imagine getting up to use the john, much less leaving to avoid her probing questions.

"My father was a Marine. As was his father before him."

"So it's a family business," Laney said.

He smiled. "Yes, I suppose you could say that."

"And your mom?"

Christ. "My mom left a long time ago. Remarried, had more kids and lives a nice, suburban life with a nice, boring husband down in Austin."

"How old were you when she left?"

Carter turned his head toward her. "What, did JAG give you an outline of questions to ask?"

She looked hurt and he immediately wanted to take his words back.

"Sorry," he said. "I guess I'm not very good at this."

"That's okay. Given your response, I'm proving I suck at it, too."

He stretched out and then brought her to lay her head

against his chest, his arm across the back of her creamy shoulders. "I was old enough to understand what was going on, young enough to be wounded for life."

"Did she try to gain custody?"

Carter scratched his eyebrow with the back of his thumbnail. "I guess she did. But my father refused to give it to her. Told her he'd drag her through court until I was eighteen and make everyone a miserable mess unless she let us alone." The images of their arguments had dulled with age, but not the biting content. "My father preferred to view her as leaving both of us."

"But surely you know that's not true."

He shrugged. Maybe he did. Maybe he didn't. At any rate, since his mother had moved three hours away, where her family had come from, he'd only seen her for a day every other weekend because his father refused to allow her to take him out of the county, even when he was away on assignment somewhere, and placed Carter with extended family members or friends. He remembered being upset that his mother hadn't fought his father. But as he grew older, he'd come to understand that you didn't fight with his father so much as ram up against an immovable force of nature. So maybe she'd understood that any legal claims she would have liked to have made would have accomplished little more than fueling bad feelings to worse.

Laney made a thoughtful sound. "So since then you've been punishing every woman who's crossed your path for your mother's sins."

Carter jerked to stare at her. "What?"

She met his gaze. "I heard the expression some-place—I don't remember where."

"Do you think I'm punishing you?"

She squinted at him, as if trying to work it out in her mind. "Not so much punishing as trying to keep me at arm's length. Sort of, 'You can come this far, but no farther.' Frankly, it's beginning to piss me off."

He chuckled softly. There was a certain fuzzy kind of logic to her words.

And a flattering aspect that touched him in ways that he was unprepared to acknowledge.

Had it really been just yesterday that he'd worked out it was best not to see her anymore? That to continue building on a relationship that held no future was in neither of their best interests?

Yet here he was, lying with her in his arms, not wanting to be anyplace else in the world.

"Is everything in your life so simple, Laney?" he asked quietly. "So ordered?"

He heard her swallow hard. "My life is no less a mess than anyone else's. No less conflicted than yours, I think."

Carter smoothed his hand down her silky back. "Then answer me this—would you be here right now, lying next to me, if someone wasn't posing a threat to you?"

THE QUESTION had been unfair. And moot.

Laney sat in her office the following morning thinking about last night. She was due in the war room in five minutes but she couldn't seem to motivate herself to reach for her coffee cup, much less devote her attention to the MacGregor case.

She understood that Carter's question was exactly what she'd accused him of—an attempt to keep her at arm's length. And she supposed it was what she deserved after giving in to the temptation to play pop psychologist.

But knowing that didn't make her hurt any less.

She hadn't answered his question. Hadn't had the heart to. She'd sensed that he'd already locked her out, shut down the conversation merely by posing the query. They'd lain silently for a while. Then Carter had gotten up to take his position on the couch, leaving Laney by herself in the big, lonely bed that smelled of him. To have him so near, yet so far away, had hurt the most.

So this was what it felt like to be falling in love. The never-ending longing, the soaring highs, the ceaseless hurt and doubt. She'd heard it said by many people, including her father, that she'd know when she met that one person meant for her. She hadn't believed it. Wanted proof and a checklist so she'd know exactly what to be on the lookout for. But it turned out that falling in love wasn't about putting your finger on the emotion and saying, "There! That's it." Instead, it was something you felt with everything that you were.

And she was falling for a guy who might not be able to return the favor.

She knew Carter felt the incredible connection beginning to form between them. Knew that when they made love there were no barriers, nothing separating them as they melded into a single entity. Knew that he held her both gently, as if afraid he might break her, and possessively, as if he might never let her go.

Could she, by sheer force of purpose, lock him out the way he had done to her? Could she turn her back on what she felt? Shut her feelings off?

She wrapped her arms around herself and shivered. She'd like to think that she couldn't. But in her highly analytical lawyer's mind, she had to acknowledge that even love was ultimately a choice. Perhaps not the person you chose to love. But how and when you expressed that love.

Or not.

"Laney?"

She blinked her secretary into focus. The older woman wore a concerned expression.

Laney gathered her files together, then realized her cheeks were damp. She turned slightly and wiped them with her fingers. "Tell the guys I'll be right there."

Violet approached the desk, then backtracked to pick up a box of tissues on the guest table. She held it out.

Laney smiled and took one. "Thanks."

"You're welcome. You know, if you want to talk about anything…" She put the box down on Laney's desk. "I know you and your father are very close, but there must be times when you need a female ear to bend."

Laney was grateful. "Thank you, Violet."

In the outer office, the phone lines were ringing off the hook. Violet finally seemed to hear them.

"Actually, Laney, I didn't come in to rustle you to the war room. I came to tell you that the media appears to have gotten wind of the threats that have been made against you in the MacGregor case. And they're storming the place now."

Laney swiveled toward the window. On the street below, three news vans nearly blocked the street as techs set up portable satellite equipment and reporters did sound checks and double-checked their hair. She was familiar with each of them. Had answered their questions dozens of times outside the courthouse during the course of other high-profile cases. But never had they come to the law offices.

"Why didn't you say anything about your tires being slashed or your apartment being broken into?" Violet had come to stand next to her.

"They know that?"

Violet stared at her. "At least when I told them I had no knowledge of the incidents, I was actually speaking the truth."

"I'm sorry, Vi. There's been so much going on with trial prep that I haven't had time to think, much less conduct my life in any sort of logical way."

Understatement of the year. Of course, she was leaving out Carter's involvement in her scattered mental and emotional state.

"Here." Violet handed her a pile of messages. "The

television reporters may be outside, but the print media are tying up the phone lines. I keep telling them you'll call back but they're determined not to take no for an answer."

Laney absently accepted the messages.

"They're all asking if the threats against you are proof that there's another person involved. Another suspect that establishes MacGregor's innocence."

15

CARTER CAUGHT WIND of the media blitz when he decided to take Laney to lunch. She'd said she'd be hitting the MacGregor case hard all day and then had a charity event to attend that night. She had chaired the event and was required to attend…with him, she hoped.

He had no intention of getting anywhere near that event, with or without a black tie. But he figured what he could do was feed her. Considering all that was going on, she probably wasn't looking after herself properly.

If his impromptu lunch plans also gave him a much-needed chance to see her, he wasn't going to admit it.

To say this morning had been awkward was an understatement. He'd awakened to Blue licking his face and Laney pulling on her suit jacket, showered and ready to leave for work. He'd been disappointed she hadn't gotten him up so they could at least catch breakfast together. But considering what had transpired the last time she woke him…well, he couldn't blame her for not wanting to do it again any time soon.

Then there was last night…

Carter parked his bike and took the bag he'd brought

out of the seat compartment. Sunglasses firmly in place, he approached the media vans. Apparently they were all doing live feeds for the twelve o'clock news. He stopped to listen to one of the spot reporters, a pretty brunette unaware of his presence as she spoke into the camera.

"An undisclosed source reports that accused murderer Devon MacGregor's attorney Laney Cartwright has received several threats warning her away from defending him. The trial gets under way on Monday. The nature of those threats are as yet unclear, but we understand that her residence was broken into yesterday and intimate articles of her clothing violently slashed."

Carter walked up to the front of the building. Surprisingly, he was immediately let up after identifying himself. Perhaps Laney had cleared him as a client? Seemed likely. All he knew was that he needed to reach her, make sure she was okay.

Who had leaked the information to the press? He suspected she wouldn't much like the personal nature of the violations to be out there for public consumption. But there was nothing he could do about that now. What he could do was offer to serve as a buffer if she decided that's what she wanted.

LANEY STOOD in the war room, determined to focus on the case and what needed to be done. Her cocounsels weren't as disciplined, however. They frequently drifted toward the windows where they could see the media gathered at the curb.

"Christ, is that CNN?" Matt said.

"CNN?" Dave replied, going to check. "Laney, CNN is here."

"On a local case? I don't think so."

"God, it's Anderson Cooper."

"Anderson Cooper?" That got even her attention.

Everything had turned surreal. One of the senior partners had called her into his office a short time ago. He'd said it was completely up to her how she chose to address the media, but she might want to take some time and consider what she said so as not to compromise the case. She'd agreed and proposed using the same "My client is innocent and I'm positive the evidence will prove that" approach in regards to the case…and offer a "No comment" on any questions that involved her personally.

First one television then another was pushed into the room by associates to supplement the flat screen already on the wall. Remotes were pressed, channels selected, and the room began filling up with the occupants of nearby offices and cubicles.

"You're famous," one of the junior attorneys said almost wistfully.

Laney's picture was flashed in the upper right-hand corner of a newscast, along with a frozen frame of the grainy image taken at the convenience store robbery and shooting, crimes that Devon MacGregor was accused of committing.

"It's not about me," she said quietly. "It's about the case."

While the vast majority of her colleagues focused on the scene offered by CNN, she was drawn to a shot that appeared to be of her apartment building. She approached the screen and everyone followed her movements as a young male reporter related the incidents surrounding the break-in.

She blinked in shock. "Where are they getting their information?"

She knew that when a case was big, certain desk sergeants and other inside police sources were known to sell information to the media for extra cash. Sometimes the prosecutor's office and even defense attorneys were known to leak information if they felt it might help their case. No judge-ordered media ban was capable of keeping everything out of the press.

But there was no media ban either on the MacGregor case...or her personal life.

Everyone turned to look at her.

"Your underwear?" one of the female associates said. "Oh, that's creepy."

Laney worked her mouth around a response, but found none forthcoming.

Thankfully Violet rushed into the room, Laney's intrepid rescuer in a yellow polyester suit.

"Ms. Cartwright, your twelve-thirty appointment has arrived."

Her appointment? She didn't have any appointments.

Still, she didn't object when Violet steered her from the room and toward the ladies'. A junior attorney was washing up inside. Violet waited until she left and then turned the lock in the door.

"Thanks," Laney said for the second time that day, already feeling better away from the spotlight.

"You're welcome."

"There isn't really a twelve-thirty, is there?" she asked as she went to a sink and patted her face with cool water.

Violet handed her a paper towel. "Nothing scheduled, but there is a certain someone waiting in your office."

"Press?"

"Do you really think I'd do that to you?"

Laney wasn't sure of anything at this point.

"But you'll find out soon enough. I just thought you should know that Harold Reasoner is downstairs now, planning on addressing the press."

"What?" Why was the senior partner doing that? And why hadn't he said anything when she spoke to him earlier?

"Mmm. My response exactly when his secretary called me. Seems he wants to warn the press of harassment laws." She snorted. "More like remind himself and everyone in Dallas that he's important."

"The coverage is wider than that. CNN is here."

"CNN?" Violet looked as if she was going to do her own share of looking out the window when they left the room.

Laney slowly patted her face, wishing she had her purse so she could touch up her makeup. She wanted to look as though none of this fazed her. Maybe it had been a mistake for her to think that she could just ignore the media, pray that they went away. Perhaps she should have addressed them the minute they pulled up to the curb.

She grimaced. Precious good that would have done since she had no plans to discuss the threats that had been made against her beyond saying they were a police matter.

"So who's in my office, then?" she asked.

She caught Violet's smile in the mirror as she stood patiently behind her. "Lunch."

CARTER NOTICED the paleness of Laney's skin as she came into the room. She probably hadn't slept well last night. Which made two of them. But he didn't have half the population of Dallas waiting outside with a microphone.

Her eyes registered surprise and then warmth when she met his gaze.

"Carter."

It was almost a sigh.

He knew in that one moment that he'd done the right thing in coming.

He handed her a cup of sweet tea and motioned for her to sit down at the table where he'd laid out a virtual barbecue buffet from his favorite rib shack on Highway 303. He tried to ignore his desire to get her out of that cold place and take her to his, protect her from the mess swirling around her. Instead, he focused on her.

"Looks like today is going to be even hotter than yesterday," he said, choosing the chair opposite her. "The hog complained the whole way over."

Laney might be within touching distancing physically, but she was a long way off from being there psychologically. She looked around the table as if incapable of identifying the objects there, her hand tightly gripping her cup.

"What?" she said, finally blinking.

Carter smiled around his mouthful of pulled pork sandwich. "The heat. I hear it's one of the hottest summers on record."

She squinted at him. "Are you really talking about the weather?"

He chuckled and pushed a paper plate of samplers toward her. There were barbecue short ribs, chicken and another pulled pork sandwich. "Eat."

She finally released the cup and sat back. "I couldn't possibly swallow a bite."

"Then talk to me about the weather."

Another squint and then she shook her head.

Carter washed down the bite with a swig from a water bottle. "I remember one summer when I was about thirteen. It was so hot, I actually tried to fry an egg on our front steps." He shook his head. "Oh, it fried all right. And then calcified. Caught hell from my father later, who wasn't amused by my little experiment."

"Maybe you should have sprayed oil on the steps first," Laney said.

There. There was the woman he wanted to pull out. "Good point. Maybe I should try it again today."

Without seeming to realize she was doing so, Laney scooted her chair closer to the table and fingered the ribs. "Just so you don't do it on my steps, be my guest."

Carter loved a woman who could eat without feeling self-conscious. Of course, he suspected that Laney still wasn't one hundred percent at the table, but since this wasn't his first meal with her, he knew she would have torn into that rib no matter what her state of mind.

"You don't have steps," he said.

"Yes, I do. Three of them. Leading straight up to the lobby."

"Those don't count. They're not your steps."

"They are too my steps. I walk over them every day when I go home."

He pointed at her with his free index finger. "That doesn't make them yours. If I should go try to fry an egg on them, it won't be you who cleans it up."

"Assuming, of course, that the doorman would let you do it in the first place."

"Bingo."

"So what you're saying, then," she continued, licking sauce from her finger before taking another bite of rib, "is that the number-one responsibility of a step owner is to clean them."

"Mmm. And sit on them. And repair any cracks on occasion so that nobody trips."

"Your steps must need a lot of attention."

Carter's chewing slowed as he grinned. "You have no idea." He pointed to the other sandwich on her plate. "You going to eat that?"

She raised her brows. "I was thinking about it."

He shrugged. "Good. Because this is the best damn barbecue in the state. Be a damn shame if you weren't enjoying it."

Laney seemed to look at the stripped rib she was eating—the third—as if she couldn't believe she'd demolished it.

She put down the bone and wiped her hands. "You…" she began.

Carter swiped his own napkin across his mouth. "Me…" he prompted.

"You're good, do you know that? Real good."

"Wasn't that in a movie somewhere?"

"Yes, I think it was. Something with De Niro in it."

"And that Crystal guy."

She nodded, popping a French fry into her mouth. *"Analyze This."*

"And *That.*"

She laughed, a sound that touched him in places he couldn't begin to draw a map to.

Someone knocked on the closed door. The secretary that had ushered Carter into the office peeked inside. "Sorry to interrupt, but Harold Reasoner is on Line One."

The color instantly drained from Laney's face again.

Carter touched Laney's hand when she moved to get up, presumably to take the call at her desk. "Tell Mr.

Reasoner that Ms. Cartwright is unavailable at the moment and that she'll talk to him as soon as she can."

Was it his imagination, or had the secretary flashed him a quick grin?

"It will be my pleasure," she said as she closed the door.

Laney looked at him in gratitude and then turned her hand over so that she was holding his.

"Come on," Carter said. "Let's get out of here."

16

LANEY KNEW that Carter's talents were many, but she would never have listed among them an ability to duck the attention of the press. He'd moved his bike to the underground parking garage, where she met him, and they pulled onto the street without a second glance from the reporters.

"They'd never look for you on the back of a hog," he'd said.

Laney hugged his back, shivering as the midday heat penetrated her skin and began warming her bones. She hadn't realized she was so cold.

She had that same sensation again of wanting him to never stop. To ride forever. Until there was no more road to follow. But this time it was for a different reason. She wanted to run away. What from, she couldn't exactly say. The story-hungry media was a given, but it was more than that. Sure, she had a difficult case. But she believed in her client's innocence. She was experiencing the usual fear that she might not succeed in her defense of him, that she might fail, but she had been through the process enough to put it down to pretrial nerves. She was a damn good attorney and would do everything in her power to prove Devon's innocence.

Then why this sense that she was missing something?

The motorcycle slowed under them, bringing the ride to an end all too soon. She lifted her cheek from where she'd pressed it against his back, realizing they were outside her apartment building. A television crew sat across the street, but as Carter had predicted, the reporters showed little interest in the classic Harley and its passenger.

The daytime doorman peered out and Carter gave him a thumbs-up. The garage door accessible only by residents slid open and he drove inside.

If Laney was disappointed that he'd brought her home, she wasn't about to share it. What had she expected? For him to read her mind and keep on riding? Or had she secretly hoped he would take her to his place?

"You okay?" he asked as she stood next to the bike and waited for him to get off.

"Huh? Oh, yes, yes. I'm fine." She looked over her shoulder to see the garage door close, completely concealing them from sight. "Thanks for this."

"No problem." He swept his leg over the motorcycle and then took the bag of take-out food from under his seat. "Now let's get this upstairs. It's a crime of the tallest order to let great barbecue like this go to waste."

CARTER DIDN'T OBJECT when Laney went to change out of her suit. And while he was surprised when he heard the shower switch on, he didn't let it deter him from setting out the food the same way he had in her office, adding to the mix a couple of beers from the fridge. When she came back out, he was just about to help himself to her pulled pork sandwich. She plucked it out from under his nose before he could take a bite.

"Go get your own, **Marine**. This is mine."

She looked miles away from the woman he'd encountered just a few blocks up. Color had returned to her face. Her hair was curlier after her shower (he guessed she must have worn a cap because she couldn't have blown it dry that fast) and the spark he was coming to know and love had returned to her lively blue eyes.

His breath froze briefly in his lungs at his casual use of the L word. Of course, he used it as part of an expression.

Oh, yeah? Then why was he reacting the way he was at the thought of it?

He took in Laney's soft tan slacks and white top. "Don't you own a pair of sweats, for God's sake?" he grumbled.

Her preference for clingy and light-colored materials that accentuated her every soft curve was enough to force a man's mind away from everything but sex.

"Sure," she said, claiming the stool next to him and taking a bite of the sandwich. "I wear them to work out all the time."

"But not to relax."

"God, no. Why would I do that?"

He shrugged and downed half his beer. "Everyone else in the western world does it."

She smiled at him around the French fry she'd just popped into her decadent mouth. "When I wear sweats, I feel I should be working out. They don't relax me at all." She openly eyed him. "Do you wear them?"

He grumbled something under his breath. She had him there. He didn't own a pair of sweats, either. But he sure as hell didn't call wearing designer duds relaxing. "You could at least put on an old pair of jeans or something."

"Here," she said, holding out the rest of her sandwich. "Apparently I've upset you. Let me offer this by way of a truce."

He accepted it, cut it into two pieces and handed her back half, which she readily took. They continued eating in silence for a few minutes. As Carter watched her face, he could tell the big, heavy wheels of her mind were turning. He could virtually hear the squeaking and nearly asked if she needed a little oil.

"So what do you make of the media onslaught?" she asked. "I mean, knowing everything that has happened so far?"

He shrugged. "I don't know. It could prove to be a good thing, right? You believe your client is innocent and these threats and attacks might be an attempt to divert attention from the real guilty party. That would help your case, wouldn't it?"

"You mean by publicizing the threats made against me, public opinion could swing to favor my client or at least raise doubt."

He nodded.

"Is it a good thing?" She chewed on the last of her fries. "I don't know. I'm not so sure." She sat back and sighed. "God, at this point the media's probably wondering if my office leaked the information."

"And did they?"

She blinked. "Not even a remote possibility. The first note aside, no one knew anything to leak."

"You didn't say anything to anyone?"

"No. There really wasn't time."

"The police, then."

She fell silent for a moment. "That seems the more likely source, but…"

He handed her a napkin. "But what?"

"But they believe MacGregor is guilty, so why leak something that might make him appear innocent?" She absently wiped her hands and then put the crumpled napkin on her empty plate. "Sure, not everyone at the DPD is political. Their own pockets are more important than a case that doesn't directly impact them, but…"

He watched her work through the possibilities. Laney was drop-dead gorgeous when she smiled at him suggestively. She was even more appealing when she was thinking about something. Her Kewpie doll mouth edged down at one corner, her blue, heavily lashed eyes squinted, her rounded chin cocked to one side.

God, he realized that he wanted to ravish her, the case and the media be damned.

"I don't know. I feel like I'm missing something. An important puzzle piece that might change everything."

"Change how?"

Her intense gaze nearly knocked the breath out of him.

"That's exactly what I don't know. And it's what scares me most."

Idle hands are the devil's playthings. So Carter busied his to keep from directing some of Laney's intensity back to him rather than her case. He gathered their empty plates and utensils together, stuffing them back into the bags in which they'd come, and then rose to throw them away.

"God! Is that the time?"

Carter looked at the microwave clock and then back at Laney, who was gaping at her watch. "I have a four o'clock appointment at my hairdresser's. And my dress has yet to be delivered."

Carter propped his hands against the counter across from her. "You aren't thinking about still going to that damn thing?"

"Of course I am. I chaired the event. My presence is required."

"Meaning that it couldn't possibly proceed without you."

"It could, but why should it?"

Carter glanced toward the windows. There was only the one media van now, but at the end of the workday the rest would certainly figure out that she was no longer in the office building and would head here, looking for footage for the six and ten o'clock newscasts.

"So you're ready to address the media, then. Have a statement prepared?"

He watched her as she followed his line of thinking, her face going pale again. "I can have something ready between then and now. Perhaps even use the coverage to help publicize the charity."

He grinned. "You're savvy, Laney. Very savvy. But have you really thought this through?"

She crossed her arms over her chest, drawing his attention to the way the clingy fabric stretched across her generous breasts. "What would you suggest?"

"I'd advise you to lay low. For at least today. Maybe tomorrow. Until the press realizes they're not going to get anything and move on to the next story."

She fell silent, apparently considering his suggestion. He guessed that she'd never had to lay low in her life. If she had appointments to get to, a charity event to attend, she would see to those responsibilities come hell or high water.

"What about your responsibility to yourself?" he asked, after voicing his thoughts. Carter pushed from the counter. "Look, Laney, the world will not end tonight if you don't go to that damn thing. But if you do go, you'll be throwing fuel onto the media fire rather than just letting it die a natural death. No matter what you say, what you do, they'll latch on to you like a pack of hungry wolves."

"Until something else comes along and they move on."

"Are you serious? All they need is five seconds of

current footage of you speaking into the camera, much less with your beautiful self decked out to the nines, and they'll crave even more. Especially now that the national media is interested. They'll be able to stretch their seconds into minutes into an hour, easy. Which means this thing doesn't end, it only intensifies."

"Which puts the focus on my client when the trial begins next week. A good thing, since I have every intention of proving his innocence."

Carter squinted at her. Was she serious? "Are you serious?"

"About his innocence?"

"No," he replied. "About your capacity to control the slant of the media. You have no idea how they'll run coverage on the trial. But I can guarantee you it will be in the direction that will grab the most attention. And that usually doesn't bode well for the character they're focused on. We've all watched murderers be turned into saints, saints into murderers for the sake of ratings."

She twisted her lips and wiped at an unseen crumb on the countertop. "What makes you such an expert?"

"I'm not. But you don't have to be one to understand that what I'm saying makes sense."

She fell silent. But he also didn't have to be a body language expert to understand that she was gearing up for a fight.

"Consider your client, Laney. Can you honestly tell me that you can live with him possibly being portrayed in a negative light—something you might have prevented just by canceling a few unimportant items on your calendar?"

"You can't say that I won't have success slanting the media the other way."

Carter took a deep breath. "No, I can't. But do you really want to take that chance?"

God, she was even more charming when she was angry. Just look at the way her plump lips pursed, her shoulders pulled back, her breasts jutted out just begging for attention.

Of course, he was relatively sure that she wouldn't welcome a kiss, much less his growing need for more. She'd likely just as soon sock him as caress him.

Then again, angry sex with the competitive Ms. Cartwright could prove interesting. Very interesting, indeed.

"I'm going to the charity event tonight, Carter." She rose from the stool and looked at her watch again. "And that's that."

He shrugged as if it were no concern of his. "Fine. Just don't get upset when I say I told you so."

He rounded the counter to stand in front of her.

"Now, tell me where I can get a tux at this late hour. Because I'm not letting you go anywhere tonight without me."

Her smile was one hundred percent pure Laney. "It's being delivered with my dress."

17

LANEY HATED TO ADMIT that Carter was right, but his predictions so far were proving to be on target. Every press van had moved from the law offices to stake out the front of her apartment building, and she'd been blinded by lights and flashbulbs as Carter accompanied her out to the limo she'd ordered a month ago. Upon his suggestion that they take his bike, she'd pointed out that even on the back of the hog, the two of them—him in a tux and her in a slinky, sequined dress—would surely catch media attention. And if it were all the same to him, she'd prefer any photos circulating in the press to be flattering, not make her look like a criminal on the lam.

Then again, better to look like a criminal on the lam than a deer caught in the headlights. She'd been unable to make out one single question in the rapid-fire onslaught of questions that met her on the front steps. She remembered saying something about the charity event, the fact that she was looking forward to proving her client's innocence when the trial got under way next week…but her tongue was glued to the back of her throat when they'd asked her about the threats against her.

"Well, that went according to plan," Carter had said casually in the back of the limo.

Now, an hour later at The Centre, she found herself staring at him as she had so often since he'd emerged from the penthouse guest room wearing the tux. She'd guessed at his measurements and was glad to see that the black fabric fit his muscular form to perfection. While he absently tugged at the starched collar of his shirt every now again, and straightened his bow tie, he looked amazingly relaxed for a man who had never attended a formal event of this nature. His dark brown hair looked handsomely disheveled, giving him a reckless playboy sort of appearance that was attracting the women in droves. Every time she left him to mingle and to see to event details, they descended on him like a flock of doves, preening and cooing, each trying to command his attention even as he looked for a mysterious someone just outside their circle. Then he'd meet Laney's gaze and she would realize that someone was her. And her stomach would pitch to the heels of her black stilettos.

What she hadn't anticipated, and neither had Carter, was that everyone she came across would be as inter-ested as the press in learning the specifics of the threats she'd received.

Without the glare of media lights, she'd been able to smile and deliver the line she'd choked on in front of the cameras. "It's a police matter now, so you'll excuse me if I can't discuss it further." Then she'd move on to the next group of donors to avoid answering their questions.

"Who's the hottie?" her friend Betsy now asked, taking her arm and leading her away from the pack.

Laney accepted a fresh glass of champagne from a passing waiter, trying to hide her smile as her gaze sought out the man in question. "Why, I don't know to whom you could possibly be referring," she said.

"Sure you don't. The guy is pissing off every other bachelor in the place, as well as a few of the roving married ones, because all the women are following him around like a bunch of groupies."

Laney laughed. "Yes, well…"

She and Betsy went back to their first day at UT. Oh, she'd always known who Betsy Ewing was. From what she understood, Betsy's family liked to pretend they were the inspiration behind the wildly popular 1980s television series, a distinction Laney couldn't fathom wanting to encourage. But even she had indulged in wondering which one was J.R. and which was Bobby with friends at events such as the one tonight.

On the first day of college, she and Betsy had become fast friends. While they always obeyed the style laws passed down by generations of Southern ladies, they also shared an unquenchable desire to achieve professional success independent of their families' wealth. Laney had focused on law with a passion, while Betsy had gone the business route.

The two of them still met regularly for what they called late-night exhaustion sessions, where they checked into a posh suite at a downtown hotel, both of them too wound up to sleep. They ordered almost every item on the room service menu, watched movies on pay-per-view, and usually but not always slept in the following day.

There had never been a need for either of them to check their tongues at the door. Unfortunately, Laney had the unsettling feeling that was about to change.

Betsy looked at her closely. "Uh-oh. Don't tell me you're dating him."

Laney knew she shouldn't ask, but she needed to. "Why?"

"Oh, Laney. By all means, you can fuck a guy like him, but you can't possibly be insane enough to date one."

Laney felt as if Betsy had just poured a drink over her head. "Oh, and just what do you think you know about him?"

"What, do you think I just got out of high school yesterday? I know this guy. And hundreds more like him. Wannabe cowboys who can't tell the difference between a good shiraz and a cabernet."

"I can choose my own wine. And he's not a cowboy, he's a Marine."

Betsy paused with her glass halfway to her mouth. "Same thing."

Laney's cheeks burned. "I think you'd better lighten up on the champagne, Bets. You don't know what you're talking about."

"I know exactly what I'm talking about. Oh, don't get me wrong. Things are nice for the first couple of months. Great, really, because these guys…mmm. They're fantastic in bed. Then the passion starts to cool and you realize that the only thing you share in common is the bathroom you use."

"That's so crass!"

Betsy shrugged. "It is what it is, Laney. And it always has been. You can take a guy off the range, but you can't take the range out of the guy. It's just the way things are. How they've always been. I can name at least ten women we both know who have made the mistake and are spending the rest of their lives paying for it."

A pudgy man in a tuxedo at least two sizes two small walked by, nearly tripping over his own feet. Barton Fogarty had married into the Cantrell family, one of the wealthiest families in the whole of Texas, thirty years ago. And while his wife appeared to grow more brittle as a result of excessive dieting and plastic surgery, her husband had turned to drink to amuse himself while she was otherwise busy.

Betsy looked at her pointedly. "Exhibit A."

Laney rolled her eyes. "You can't possibly compare Queenie Cantrell's marriage to a ranch hand to Carter and me."

"Can't I?"

Laney's throat almost refused to swallow her champagne.

"Take my advice, Laney. Screw him as long as you like. Then dump him. But promise me you won't make any decisions beyond the next sack session. Please."

"God, I can't believe what a snob you are," Laney said under her breath.

Betsy's date came up and took her by the arm. Laney raised her brows as she realized it was Jason Gaston, a high-profile business attorney from old money that Laney herself had dated a couple of times.

Her friend's smile was nothing if not predatory. "You remember Jason, don't you, Laney?"

She managed to exchange a few pleasantries with him and then the couple walked off, likely to crow about what a great power couple they made and ponder the lifelong mistake Laney might be on the verge of making.

She looked for Carter's handsome face in the crowd, suddenly feeling sick to her stomach. She found him near the buffet table pulling at his collar even as he piled shrimp on a plate.

"SO, MR. SOUTHARD, what is it that occupies your time?" a certain Miss Texas U asked, batting lashes the length of his finger.

An hour into the event and Carter had been approached no fewer than a dozen times by what he was coming to think of as the Dallas Debutante Society. He'd stopped trying to remember names and instead labeled them in a way that differentiated one from the next. Miss Magnolia for her white-and-pink dress, Miss Stone for the diamonds dripping from her every limb, and now Miss UT, who looked as if she might break into a cheer any second, or jump behind the bleachers with him if he made the suggestion.

"I'm chairman of the very successful dot-com hoodoo," he said, offering up another in a long line of answers he'd given to each of the women even as he visually searched for the only woman in the room important to him…and the only woman who knew the truth about him and what he did.

And that's the way he intended to keep it.

"If you'll excuse me…" He almost called her Miss UT. "Daisy."

"Of course, Daisy," he continued. "I see that my presence is being requested elsewhere."

The young brunette looked put out and made no secret of her curiosity as she craned her neck to see who he had come with.

Laney's blue eyes flashed at him warmly as he crossed the room. She took a long sip of champagne and his attention moved to her red, pouty lips.

"So, Mr. Southard, how does it feel to have every eye in the place on you tonight?" she asked when he reached her.

He gave her an open once-over that seemed to embolden her as she thrust a bare shoulder forward and tilted her head, sending him a look that could only be described as come-hither.

"I beg to differ, Ms. Cartwright," he said. "Every eye is on you and that shockingly sexy backless dress you have on."

Her laugh was low but full of spunk.

"You're proving quite popular tonight," she said after briefly greeting a couple passing by.

Carter put his hand in his jacket pocket to prevent himself from pulling at his too-tight collar yet again. He felt something and pulled it out to find two business cards, likely slipped there by the women he'd met.

"You have no idea," he grumbled, putting the cards on the tray of the first waiter that passed by.

"Discover any interesting prospects?" Laney asked.

"That depends." Damn, she was sexy. The most beautiful woman in the room.

"Oh? On what?"

He leaned in closer to her, wrapping his fingers around her bare upper arm. "On whether or not you plan on propositioning me," he whispered into her ear.

He felt her shiver and then she drew back to smile at him. "Let's say your place? In an hour?"

His place.

Carter grimaced and removed his hand.

After tonight's media circus, he knew that going back to her place wouldn't be an option. But neither was going to his, for more reasons than he cared to explain, given their present company.

"I was thinking something a little more…conducive to what I have in mind," he said instead.

"Oh. What is it, Mr. Southard? Are you hiding a wife at home?" she asked.

He chuckled. "Just an old hound dog that thinks my bed is his when I'm away."

"I think I've learned to live with a little dog slobber over the past couple of days."

Carter accepted a glass of bourbon from a passing waiter and sipped at the fiery liquid. "I'm thinking more along the lines of a hotel. Preferably one with a hot tub."

He had to give her credit for not voicing the disappointment that slipped across her face. "Sounds illicit."

"You have no idea."

Now, if he could only talk her into getting the hell out of there within the next five minutes, maybe he could get back to a place where he didn't feel like a damn penguin a thousand miles away from the nearest block of ice.

18

TWO HOURS LATER, Laney led Carter through what she said was one of her favorite places growing up: the horse stables on her father's estate.

Carter had been under no illusions when it came to her family's wealth. But he could never have imagined the expansive compound a half hour outside Dallas where she'd been raised. The house sat back nearly a quarter of a mile from the road, looking more like a sprawling three-story hotel than a single-family home. The garage alone was larger than most people's houses, and he counted at least seven bay doors that hid, he had little doubt, seven high-end cars.

He tried to imagine the long, black stretch limo that had brought them there pulling up outside his two-bedroom shack. Here, it was right at home, cruising up the long, circular drive and coming to a stop in front of double doors that looked large enough to drive a Mack truck through.

But rather than take him straight inside the house, she'd led him to the stables some way off to the right. The darkness cloaked much of the opulence of his surroundings, he was sure, but the estate was well lit, allowing him to take in the enormous stables and extensive landscaping.

Christ, his military pay over the course of a year probably wasn't enough to cover the upkeep of this place for a week.

He watched Laney walk ahead of him. She still wore her slinky black dress but had taken off her heels, letting the straps dangle from the index finger of her left hand as she moved like a sexy ghost through stables that, if he wasn't mistaken, were built of mahogany or some equally expensive wood.

Hell, the place was so top-shelf, he wondered how the horses dared drop a load on the pristine, straw-covered floor.

Laney placed her right hand on top of a carved stall door that bore a brass nameplate and turned to face him, her smile lighting her pretty face.

"Song, there's someone I'd like you to meet," she said.

The head of a black Arabian poked over the top of the door. The horse whinnied and then sat still as Laney stroked his long, shiny nose.

Carter leaned against the connecting wall. He'd taken off the blasted bow tie and stuffed it into his pocket the instant they'd climbed into the limo and then had undone a few of the top buttons of the scratchy shirt, but he was a long way from feeling comfortable, a condition not helped by their current surroundings.

"Is there something I should shake?" he asked with a raised brow.

Laney laughed softly. "I've had Song for ten years. My father named him that because he said that's what he bought him for—a song."

She quoted an amount that could probably buy the rights to one of Michael Jackson's albums.

Carter reached out and allowed the horse to smell his hand, then ran his palm over the horse's solid neck. He hadn't been around horses much other than the neighbor's broken-down beast who liked to graze in his overgrown backyard every now and again. But obviously Laney was right at home talking baby talk to the great stallion and feeding him sugar cubes she took from a nearby bag that hung on the wall.

"Does your father breed horses?" he asked.

"Dad? No. He did for a couple of years when I was younger, but horses were more my mother's passion than my father's." She absently patted the horse. "He sires out a couple of the stallions, like Song here, but that's the extent of his interest. And even then, the stable manager sees to the details."

She drew in a deep breath, bringing his attention to her long, elegant throat and the modest diamond-and-amethyst necklace she wore. "I love the smell of the stables."

Carter twisted his lips. "Depends on how recently they've been cleaned."

He got the feeling these stables were cleaned twice

a day by a manager and hands who likely lived on the premises.

"Come on," Laney said. "Let's go inside the main house so I can show you around."

"How many houses are there?"

"Not including staff accommodations? Four."

He'd been joking when he asked the question. So he didn't quite know what to do with the answer.

"Dad says it's important for guests to feel at home when they visit. So he makes sure they have their own houses, complete with working staff and transportation."

"Transportation meaning…"

"Cars."

Carter was suddenly all too aware that he didn't have his bike here. In fact, as good as he could figure it, he was stuck at the Cartwright mansion and completely at Laney's mercy when it came to getting back to town. He didn't think taxis responded to calls this far out. And as far as he could tell, the nearest neighbor was a mile up the road and their place looked about as welcoming as this one did. If he knocked on their door unannounced, he'd likely find a police cruiser summoned for his transportation.

It might just be worth escaping this parallel universe of lavish excess.

He was slightly grateful that Laney led him around to the back of the house instead of the front. He held the door she opened and then followed her inside what could be considered a mudroom but was the size of his living room. Raincoats neatly hung on hooks and various boots were lined up along the wall, with two benches to sit on. He noticed that she didn't even have to click on any light switches. It was as though a spotlight followed her wherever she stepped.

Welcome to the lives of the wealthy, he thought wryly.

She dropped her shoes in the hall and walked into a kitchen large enough to cater half the city.

"This was always my favorite room in the house," she said, washing her hands at the sink. He followed suit and accepted the towel she offered. "Are you hungry? I could probably rustle us up some leftovers. Or there are always sandwich fixings."

Rustle...fixings...Carter couldn't help his grin. Somewhere along the line someone had injected a dose of everyday Texas expressions into her life. He wondered who. Did she hang around the stables when she was a kid? Had the housekeeper or cook played a big role in her life?

"I could go for a sandwich," he said.

A stout, middle-aged woman in a maid's uniform appeared in the doorway, presumably from a back stairway or servants' quarters. She looked as if it were seven in the morning, rather than midnight, and she was clocking in for the day.

"Good evening, Miss Laney. Shall I prepare something for you?"

Laney greeted the woman warmly. "No, thank you, Gladys. We can take care of ourselves. Sorry to have woken you."

"No apologies necessary. Let me know if you need anything."

"We'll be fine. I'll see you in the morning."

Carter watched the woman disappear as silently as she'd appeared. He sat down at one of six stools positioned around a prep island as large as a car, running his hand over the dark, smooth granite. The room was brightly lit, displaying all its over-the-top glory. Was that a pizza oven in a small room off to his right? Laney opened a cabinet to reveal a series of switches, and experimented until just a couple of the soft lights in the ceiling shone on the island and above the sink. She smiled at him as she walked over to the refrigerator.

Damn. His face must have given away his uneasiness with his surroundings. But even the dimmed lighting couldn't hide the fact that he was in way over his head here. While this house might be Laney's home, he couldn't imagine ever taking a place like this for granted. Or remembering the times when his father had been stationed overseas and he'd faced bare cupboards.

He absently rubbed the back of his neck, surprised when Laney slid a plate in front of him holding one of the largest sandwiches he'd ever seen.

She laughed. "My father always says that if you're going to make a sandwich, there's no reason why you shouldn't make a good one."

She filled a couple of bowls with chips and pretzels and came to sit next to him, her sandwich a much more modest version of his own.

Damn, but she was beautiful.

He took a deep breath, feeling some of the tension seep from his muscles as he looked at her. What a fascinating creature she was, sitting there in bare feet, designer gown, a smear of mayonnaise at the side of her mouth as she took a bite of her sandwich.

Carter tilted her chin up with his fingers and wiped the mayo away with a swipe of his thumb.

"Drinks!" Laney said, appearing suddenly antsy. "I forgot to get us something to drink."

Carter squinted at her. So not all was well with the only child of the house, either. Interesting...

"Do you bring many guys home?" he asked, trying for casual as he took a bite of his sandwich.

Laney didn't answer right away. Instead, she asked him if beer was all right and he nodded.

"Actually, outside my senior year prom date, you're the first."

That got his attention. "Any specific reason?"

She shrugged. "I don't know... Until now it never struck me as odd. But when I was working toward getting my law degree, there seemed to be so little time to develop a strong enough relationship with a guy I would want to bring home."

Carter reminded himself that the only reason she'd brought him here was because of the press nipping at her heels.

"Besides, Dad and I are so close that when I came home, I did it for the express reason to spend time with him." She smiled. "Another person would have detracted from that."

"Ah, a daddy's girl."

She drew her shoulders back. "And proud of it."

They fell into an easy silence, and before Carter knew it, he'd polished off his sandwich along with half of hers and had drained his beer bottle.

"Good?" she asked.

"Great."

"Good."

Was it him, or did Laney suddenly seem uncomfortable?

Damn, he wished more than ever he had his bike here. Because this was exactly the point where he'd wish her a good-night and take off.

Instead, he felt like he was going to end up as that detraction.

"Where is your father?" he asked, looking around. Somehow he got the feeling that if Mr. Cartwright were here, he'd have made his presence known already.

Laney shifted on her stool. "He's out of town until tomorrow morning. Some trip up to Alaska to see about an invention that converts natural gas to hydrogen."

He nodded. "Of course."

"So…" she said.

"So."

"Um, it's after midnight. Shall I show you to your room?"

"I have a room?"

She laughed, and Carter realized that she was as uncomfortable about the sleeping arrangements as he was.

"Lead on," he said with a sweep of his arm after they'd cleaned up after themselves.

Laney did. Across a half acre of the first floor, up the sweeping staircase, and on to the second floor, which very much resembled the upscale hotel he'd compared the outside to.

She stopped in front of a door and then opened it, switching on a light. "This is one of the guest rooms that are always kept prepped."

He stepped inside, took in the king-size bed, the mammoth flat-screen TV, the fireplace.

He turned toward her. Was it his imagination, or had she just backed up a step?

"My room's in the east wing."

"Ah. Let me guess. A long way from this room."

She smiled and looked down at her feet. "I'm sorry… It's just that even at my age, this will always be my father's house…"

Carter stepped closer to her, cupping her face in his right hand. "It's all right. I can understand your need to respect him."

Her expression of relief was so profound that he couldn't help leaning in to kiss her.

Laney sighed against him, melting into his arms as he threaded his fingers in her hair, shaking the soft strands free of the pins holding them in place.

Moments later, they pulled apart, Carter's breathing

ragged. "I think you'd, um, better go before I have a change of heart."

She nodded and walked backward toward the door, nearly tripping over the hem of her dress. "All right. Um, I'll see you in the morning."

"Good night."

The door clicked closed and Carter turned back toward the bed. He was better off spending the night alone. In a place like this, he was afraid even a man like him could come down with a massive case of performance anxiety.

19

CARTER WOKE to the sun slanting in through the window. He jackknifed to a sitting position in the bed, squinting at his surroundings before picking up the clock on the nightstand.

Seven-thirty.

Damn.

After Laney had left him alone, he'd been convinced he wouldn't be able to sleep a wink, but he must have drifted off shortly after having the thought, just now awakening to an empty room.

He tossed the blankets to the other side of the bed and sat scrubbing his face with his hands, wondering how he'd gotten into such a mess. He…Laney… They weren't just from different classes, they lived on different planets.

He looked up to find a pile of clothing on the dresser. He got up and read the note on top. "In case you'd like a change of clothes, Mr. Carter," it read. He fingered through the choices of jeans and shirts, and noticed where a few pairs of casual shoes had also been left. All of them still bore price tags.

Christ, they kept clothes on hand?

He shook his head and walked into the connecting bathroom, catching a quick shower before putting on the tux from the night before, minus the jacket. He rolled up the shirtsleeves, then went in search of life.

He found it in the kitchen.

He'd suspected the night before that the darkness had prevented him from seeing the room and the estate as they really were, but he was still unprepared for the reality. Through the back windows, he saw land that stretched on forever, a series of lush, manicured paddocks, an Olympic-sized pool, what looked like a dirt bike track complete with death knolls and carefully positioned gates.

"Good morning!"

The sound of Laney's voice jarred him out of his thoughts. She got up from a long table to his right that overlooked a large deck. The man with her was no doubt her father, and he was looking at Carter with a mixture of wariness and amusement.

Laney was dressed in riding apparel, complete with boots, as was her father. Had they already been out?

Even as Laney kissed him on the cheek and took his arm, he couldn't help feeling put out. Why hadn't she woken him?

She led him toward the table. Her father wiped his mouth with his napkin and then stood.

"Daddy, I'd like you to meet Carter Southard. Carter, this is my father, Blake Cartwright."

"A pleasure, Mr. Cartwright," Carter said. "This is some place you've got here."

"It's Blake, please. And thank you."

"We were just having breakfast. Won't you join us?" Laney asked.

Carter wanted to say no, ask her to take him into town pronto, away from this strange existence back to a place that was more familiar, but he realized he couldn't. Unless he jumped on the back of one of the horses he could see being led into the stables, he was stuck for now.

"Thank you," he said, sitting next to Laney and across from the elder Cartwright.

Thankfully father and daughter appeared to have finished with their meal so Carter accepted a breakfast roll and a cup of black coffee and uneasily traded casual conversation on the weather and riding.

"Well, I think I'm going to grab a shower and get dressed," Laney said finally, getting to her feet again. Carter rose, as did her father, to acknowledge her departure. "Will you be ready to leave in twenty?" she asked Carter.

He wanted to ask if ten was out of the question. Or why she couldn't just take him right now.

Instead, he nodded. "Twenty minutes is fine."

Carter watched her leave, appreciating the way her riding pants fit her rounded bottom. Then he realized he was checking out her ass in the presence of her father. Not the smartest of moves.

"Come, Carter. Let's go out onto the deck," Blake Cartwright said.

He opened a door that had no handle as far as Carter could tell, then motioned for him to walk through. The two men stood side by side holding their coffee cups, looking out over the vast tract of land.

"Do you mind if I just cut through the bullshit and come straight to the point, Carter?"

He blinked at the older man, immediately respecting the way he did business.

"I wouldn't have it any other way."

Blake looked at him squarely. "Don't let your current surroundings fool you. If you hurt my little girl, I will come gunning for you, Mr. Southard. Military training or no."

Carter held his gaze for a long moment, and then finally nodded. "I would feel no differently if I had a daughter, Mr. Cartwright."

Blake stared at him and then seemed to come to the conclusion that he'd been understood. "Very good, then." He grinned. "Now, Laney tells me we share an interest in motorcycles. Why don't we take a walk down to the dirt bike track?"

EARLY THE FOLLOWING Monday morning, Laney sat in her office, barely aware that the sun had yet to rise outside her window. It was barely 6:00 a.m., but the office buzzed with activity. Or at least her end of it, as she and her cocounsel, assistants and paralegals prepared for the MacGregor trial, which would begin in just under three hours.

"Did you sleep last night?" Violet asked, bringing in a cup of coffee.

Laney gave her a long look.

"Right. Neither did I. I kept thinking I'd forgotten to copy the witness depositions, and then when I did finally fall asleep, I dreamed that I'd fed them to the shredder instead of the copy machine and there were no other copies anywhere to be had."

Laney smiled. "I dreamed I was strapped to a table and being administered a lethal injection."

Violet raised her hands. "Okay, on the creepiness scale, you win."

"Small comfort."

Laney leaned her head against her hand and sipped the hot coffee, allowing the strong liquid to surge through her veins, feeding her much-needed caffeine.

"Has the process delivery receipt come back yet on Tiffany Mullins?" she asked.

Violet narrowed her eyes. "I put it on your desk."

Laney moved papers around and came up with it. "So you did."

Thankfully, Violet didn't say what she was obviously thinking as she collected a pile of folders from the out-box, some of which were the original copies of depositions featured in her dream.

"Let me know if you need anything," Violet said.

"I will. Thanks."

Okay, so maybe her sleepless night had more to do with Carter than with pretrial jitters. She'd rewritten her opening statement no fewer than five times over the past few hours. About as many times as she'd found her hand reaching for the phone, yearning to call Carter.

She hadn't seen him since she'd driven back to her apartment the other morning after they spent the night at her father's house. She'd chattered about inane topics all during the drive, feeling suddenly awkward in his company for reasons she couldn't quite pinpoint. Or, rather, feeling suddenly uncomfortable with his reaction to her.

He'd sat back and stared out the window, contributing little to the conversation. And the more silent he became, the more she'd talked.

Truth was, she'd felt uncomfortable when she'd viewed the Cartwright estate through his eyes. It had always been home to her, but for a few brief, unwanted moments it had looked like a horrible example of excess, especially in these difficult economic times.

How must he have viewed her in those surroundings? How must he have judged her father?

Of course, she understood that the family money had been earned through the hard work of her great-grandfather and grandfather, then multiplied by her father, but how much did one family need?

Laney shook off the uneasy feelings. Never, ever, had she experienced anything like it. So when Carter had said goodbye to her in the garage, climbed onto the back of his Harley and driven away, she didn't try to stop him. She was almost relieved he was going.

And she'd been haunted by the image and the memory ever since. Along with a dull achy need that refused to go away, no matter how busy she kept herself.

She picked up the process server receipt. She'd requested and had been granted a Subpoena to Appear to one antagonistic Ms. Tiffany Mullins. Her cocounsel Dave Matthews had questioned the move. One of the first rules in the defense attorney handbook was never to ask a witness a question that you didn't already know the answer to.

At this point in the case, after suffering through three threats and conflicting information, Laney decided she just wanted answers.

Besides, she didn't expect Tiffany would get anywhere near the courthouse. Girls like her didn't earn the rap sheet they did by obeying the law.

No. Laney's intentions were to scare a few birds out of the bushes and see what happened. She glanced at her watch. Problem was, time was running out and the birds appeared to be clinging to the bush.

CARTER SAT in a coffee shop just up the street from Laney's offices. While he didn't expect her to recognize his bike, he wasn't taking any chances and had parked it a block over. Far enough to keep her from knowing he was watching out for her. Close enough to intervene if someone did try to pull something.

"More coffee, sweetheart?" a pretty, young wait-ress asked.

He pushed the cup in her direction and continued to stare out the window.

He hadn't meant to be as cold as he was the other day. Laney hadn't deserved that. But his emotions had been too raw. She may have come from a place where every-thing was put on the table, but he'd been raised that emotions were best kept to yourself. Where talking was thought to be overrated and it was what a man did that defined him, not what he said.

He grimaced as he sipped his coffee. He bet that Laney and her father talked about everything under the sun.

He remembered Blake Cartwright's words to him.

Hurt my little girl, and I'll come gunning for you.

It was then that Carter understood what he had to do. He had to end things with Laney before they went too far. Before he ended up hurting her more than she would be already.

Before he ended up hurting himself more, even though that seemed impossible given his own pain, which was like a hunting knife to the chest.

He cleared his throat and pressed both hands against his coffee cup.

There was no future for them. His world was foreign to her. Her world was another planet, inhabited by aliens who could drop a hundred grand on a bike track in the backyard that was barely used just because they woke up with the idea one morning, but had yet to actually ride on it.

Impossible. That's what any thought of a future relationship with Laney seemed like to him.

And in case he needed proof, all he had to do was remember the details of his own parents' failed marriage.

Oh, his mother's family wasn't anywhere near as wealthy as the Cartwrights. But just enough to make his father feel like less of a man. Just enough to cause love to turn to bitterness.

Christ, his father would love this. Like father, like son. He'd ended up making the exact same mistake as his dad.

Well, almost. By stopping it now, at least he wouldn't be hurting any children.

A vision of a young boy with his mom's pale blond hair and his dad's hunger for adventure riding over that hundred-thousand-dollar track filled his mind.

He rubbed his closed eyelids with the pads of his index fingers. Now he was seeing things that would never be.

But the fact that he'd even thought about children with Laney was momentous. Because he'd never considered them before beyond a niggling fear that the condom might have broken and he'd impregnated someone he'd never had any intention of marrying.

Yet with Laney…

He shoved his coffee cup aside, causing liquid to spill over the side and the cup to clatter against the saucer. He really needed to stop this adolescent bullshit. He wasn't some damn kid wet behind the ears. He was a thirty-year-old man who certainly knew when to climb off a ride that wasn't fun anymore.

But what was a man to do when all he could think about was that damn ride?

There was movement in front of the office building.

Carter focused on a motorcycle that had just pulled up to the curb. Not a Harley like his, but one of those newfangled racing bikes, yellow, with the driver dressed all in black, including a helmet with a mirrored visor. But it wasn't the driver who caught his attention; it was his passenger. A girl of about eighteen or nineteen, wearing a short black leather skirt and a neon-green belly tank, got off the back of the bike. She pulled the large bag hanging behind her around to her front, then turned away from the lobby of the building. Hunching over slightly, she took something out of the bag, seeming to check it.

Carter realized it was a gun.

He took out a twenty-dollar bill and flicked it to the table.

"Hey, mister! Don't you want your change?" the waitress called after him.

Carter ignored her. He was too busy cursing himself for being so far away from the building. Too far away to stop the young woman packing heat from entering. Too far away to stop her from doing whatever it was she planned to do.

20

LANEY PACKED the last of the exhibits in a large, vinyl carrying case. This was it. Everything was ready to go. Even now, her client, Devon MacGregor, was being transferred to the courthouse lockup. And whether she was prepared or not, in little more than an hour the trial would begin.

She stood near her office window, hands on hips, and let out a long sigh. Down on the curb she spotted a motorcycle. Her heart skipped a beat. Until she realized that it wasn't Carter.

She watched one of the lobby guards come out of the building and head in the biker's direction. The rider took off in a squeal of tires and a loud roar she could hear even at this height.

"All set?" Dave asked, collecting the carrying case from her desk.

Laney turned from the window. "All set. All we have left to do now is pray."

"I thought that's what we do when the case goes to the jury."

She smiled. "I tend to do it through the entire process." She put her briefcase and purse on her desk. "I figure it can't hurt."

"Good point. Meet you there?"

She nodded. "See you there."

She watched Dave leave. Violet followed after him toward the elevators, loading him down with even more case materials.

Laney plucked her suit jacket from the back of her chair and turned toward the window again as she shrugged into it. She didn't know what she was looking for, but she couldn't help herself from looking nonetheless.

"Stay right where you are, lawyer bitch."

Laney slowed her movements, making out the figure of the young woman in the glass. She was pointing something at her as she closed the door to the office. Laney had little doubt that something was a gun.

She hadn't anticipated the gun.

But the girl's appearance was exactly what she'd hoped for.

She slowly shifted to face her, holding her hands slightly up in the air. "Hi, Tiffany," she said as calmly as she could. "You're late."

The girl looked over her shoulder at the closed door and then back again. "What are you talking about?"

Laney pulled out her chair. "Why don't we sit down—"

"Look who thinks she's calling the shots!" Tiffany waved the gun. "See this here? This tells me I'm the one in charge."

"I didn't mean to imply otherwise."

"Sit down. And if there's any kind of silent alarm or something, don't you dare touch it. Not if you don't want to see blood all over that pretty white suit you're wearing."

"I wouldn't dream of it."

"Why did you say I'm late?"

Laney shrugged as she carefully took her seat. There was no silent alarm button. This wasn't a bank office, it was a law firm. And this was the first time to her knowledge that any of the lawyers had had a gun pointed at them in their own office.

She cleared her throat. While this wasn't going down quite as she'd expected, it didn't mean it was a lost cause. So long as she kept her wits about her.

She said as calmly as possible, "I expected to see you twenty minutes after the subpoena was served."

The girl's eyes narrowed, the gun shaking along with her hand. Laney realized she was more at risk of an accidental shooting than a purposeful one. Not exactly the mark of a girl who was used to pulling guns on people.

Then again, hadn't she learned to stop indulging in basic psychology with Carter?

Hopefully this wouldn't end up as horribly wrong as that had.

"So all this was some sort of ploy to force me out of hiding?"

"No, Tiffany. This was all some sort of ploy to get you to admit that Devon didn't rob that convenience store or kill that clerk. You did."

The girl laughed, a hysterical sound that set Laney's teeth on edge. The door swung quickly open behind Tiffany, catching her side and sending her reeling. But not before the gun she held discharged, sending a bullet whizzing in Laney's direction.

Laney dove for the floor, unsure if she'd been hit. She didn't hurt anywhere. That was a good sign, wasn't it? She glanced up to see that the bullet had hit the glass wall, leaving a tiny hole and a starburst of lines ringing it.

She crawled to peek around the desk. Carter stood over the girl and twisted the gun easily from her hand.

She'd never been so glad to see anyone in her life.

HALF AN HOUR LATER at the courthouse, Laney stood outside the basement holding cells rubbing her arms. Despite the weather report that predicted today to be one of the hottest on record, she couldn't seem to warm up.

"Are you sure you're okay?" Carter asked her.

Carter.

She didn't have to ask. Although it had felt as if he'd abandoned her, he'd been watching after her all along. She understood now that he was that kind of guy.

She also understood that despite his concern for her, he had effectively locked her out.

She nodded, although she felt anything but okay. "Thanks to you, I'm fine." She smiled without humor. "The next time I accuse someone of murder, remind me not to do it when they're holding a gun."

Carter reached out and touched the side of her face. Amazing how she immediately warmed under his fingertips. And how the small gesture inspired hope that not all was lost.

A buzzer sounded and the metal security door swung open. "You're clear to enter, Ms. Cartwright," an armed guard said.

She turned to look at Carter. Would he still be there when she finished what she had to do? She didn't know. And the prospect of his leaving frightened her more than the coming meeting.

"Ma'am?" the guard prompted.

Laney had no choice but to turn away from Carter and go talk to her client before the trial began in fifteen minutes.

She was led into a meeting room. Devon tried to stand, his hand and ankle shackles clattering. She didn't tell him not to bother. She waited until the door was closed behind her and remained standing.

"I'm going to request a dismissal," she said.

Devon blinked at her. "What?"

Laney approached the table and sat down opposite him, her movements measured to delay her response. "I'm going to request a dismissal on the grounds that the real perpetrator has been arrested."

Devon slumped back into his seat. "What?" he said again. Laney got the impression that he wasn't so much asking her the question but himself.

"Yes." Laney opened her briefcase and pretended

she needed to refer to her notes. "A Ms. Tiffany Mullins was taken into custody a short while ago."

"But that's impossible."

Laney put her hands on top of the pad. "She's already admitted to writing me threatening notes, slashing my tires and breaking into my home."

As a criminal defense attorney, Laney was used to playing her cards close to her chest. But this time one wrong card, and her entire plan would collapse.

"Is something the matter, Devon?" she asked. "I understand that Tiffany is your girlfriend—something I had to find out from someone else, I feel compelled to point out. But surely you knew her past."

"What's her past got to do with the present?"

Laney tilted her head. "Are you saying she didn't commit the robbery and shoot the clerk?"

Devon's mouth audibly snapped shut.

Throughout the course of the case, Laney had always felt she was missing something. A puzzle piece that floated just beyond her reach. And despite the bullet aimed in her direction a short time ago, she'd finally been able to grasp the bit of mystery and examine it until it made perfect sense.

When she'd met Tiffany, she'd suspected the girl had been behind the threatening notes and actions demanding that Laney drop Devon's case. But seeing that she was his girlfriend, it didn't make sense that she would want one of the best defense attorneys to leave her boyfriend hanging.

The simple explanation was that she had wanted him to hang for a crime she committed. But Laney didn't like simple. It was too neat.

Instead, she'd figured out that Tiffany had been following orders. Orders made by the boyfriend who sat across from Laney now.

She began to get up.

"Wait! Where are you going?" Devon demanded.

"To present my request to the judge in his quarters."

"But…Tiffany didn't do it."

It was a start, but not exactly what she was looking for. And seeing as the clock was ticking, she didn't have much time to get what she needed.

"So if Tiffany didn't do it, Devon, who did?"

"Whatever I say to you doesn't go beyond this room, right?"

"Attorney-client privilege."

"Tiffany didn't do it because I did it."

Bingo.

"So the threats…"

"Were supposed to throw a shadow of reasonable doubt on my case."

Just as she'd suspected. "So your idea was to convince the public that someone out there, someone who might be the real shooter, was responsible for the threats."

"Yes."

He looked all too pleased with himself. Which made what she had to say next less difficult.

She began to get up again. "Then it's my advice to you, as your attorney, that you take the prosecutor's plea deal."

"What?"

"You're guilty. Plead it."

The look on his face was one of absolute shock.

"That's my advice to you, Devon."

His mouth worked around words she couldn't make out. Then he said, "You can't do that. You have to represent me. You can be disbarred if you don't."

Laney remembered the fear she'd felt when she'd discovered her slashed tires…her ransacked apartment… when Tiffany had held the gun on her only this morning. Just so a bored kid of means could get his rocks off robbing a convenience store and shooting the clerk.

She pressed her hands against the table and leaned toward him. "Do you really want to stick with your not-guilty plea? Do you want me to represent you in a drawn-out trial, Devon? If you do, I will. But rest assured, the little stunt you tried to play on me? It will be nothing in comparison to what I can do to you."

"But you're my attorney. You're supposed to represent me no matter what."

She straightened to a standing position and crossed her arms. "Trust me, Devon, I will. But mark my words, you will still go down for this. An innocent man was murdered. Do you really expect me to overlook that?"

She shook her head and then checked her watch.

"You have five minutes to make up your mind, Devon. My advice is that you take the plea deal."

Then she left the room.

"I THINK YOU SHOULD HAVE BEEN a homicide detective instead of an attorney," Carter said after the court business was done.

Devon had ultimately taken her advice and would be serving a twenty-five-year-to-life sentence for armed robbery and second-degree murder.

She and Carter had gone to a diner afterward and sat across from each other, Dallas rushing by outside the large, picture window. While they were talking about the morning's events, something even larger loomed between them. Something that neither of them dared bring up. Something neither one of them could ignore.

"What, and throw away my law degree?" Laney said.

He considered her over the rim of his coffee cup as he drank, his eyes full of emotion.

Laney had to look away. "Not that that will be worth much after this morning is over. A senior partner has requested my presence in his office immediately."

Carter's cup clanked against his saucer as he put it down. "Shouldn't you be getting back to work, then?"

Her heart expanded in her chest. She didn't want this moment to end. She yearned to draw out this brief respite from reality as long as she could.

"What, so I can rush my resignation?" She shook her head. "I'll do it when I'm good and ready."

She supposed she couldn't really blame Harold Reasoner. Devon was his godson and the only child of his best friend. It was natural that he would want to protect Devon.

She wondered if his view would change if he knew what she did.

Then again, she suspected it wouldn't. If Devon had been found guilty as a result of trial, the firm would have lobbied heavily for him to serve his sentence at a mental facility rather than in prison, and an appeal would have been filed immediately.

This way, a bit of justice had been served. And Devon would probably still end up in a mental facility, although it would take some fancy legal maneuvering. But his father had the kind of money that could make it happen.

She shifted uncomfortably in her chair, coming closer to the something that hovered between her and Carter than she was prepared to admit.

"You're leaving the firm?" Carter asked quietly.

Laney looked down and nodded.

"What will you do?"

She shrugged. "I honestly don't know."

She took a deep breath and then exhaled, feeling better than she had in a long, long time when it came to her career. Even a week ago, uttering those words would have sent the fear of God through her. Now…well, now she'd been given a different glimpse of her future. And she needed to pursue it. At least where it pertained to her work life.

As for her personal life…

"And you?" she asked quietly. "Are you going to meet the Corps requirements and petition to be reinstated?"

Carter looked out the window. "I don't know."

Laney's cell phone vibrated in her jacket pocket. She didn't want to answer it. Didn't want to let the outside world back in just yet.

She slipped it out and reluctantly eyed the display. Violet. It was the fifth time in as many minutes that her secretary had tried to get through to her.

"I really should be getting back," she said softly.

Carter nodded, and then squinted at her as if through a cloud of smoke.

Laney took his hand before he could get up. She wanted to say something, anything, to get him to agree to meet her later. To try to work things out between them.

Instead, she whispered, "Thank you."

Carter looked as if he'd wanted her to say something different. Perhaps the words she'd been considering. "Just so everything worked out okay."

She smiled a watery smile. "Yes. I guess it has, hasn't it? On both sides."

If only she could convince her heart of the same.

21

IT HAD BEEN a long time since Carter had made this drive. And he wasn't all that clear why he was doing it now. But at some point over the past month since he'd left Laney standing outside that Dallas coffee shop, he'd begun questioning the decisions he'd made in his life so far. And one of the biggest was his decision to allow his estrangement from his mother to go on.

His old pickup truck ate up the road between Dallas and Austin. It was September now, and the heat wave might have let up, but it was still hotter than hell. He reached over and patted Blue where he sat with his head out the window, blessing those cars behind them with the gobs of slobber the wind knocked free from his sagging jowls. Taking the truck rather than his bike allowed him to bring Blue along. The old dog seemed to appreciate the gesture. The neighbor's five-year-old kid had discovered that his blunt-edged scissors cut more than colored construction paper, and Blue had the bald spots to prove it.

Oh, Carter knew that the estrangement from his mother was all his doing. She still wrote him a letter once a month, called on holidays and his birthday, and kept up on his goings-on. Without fail, she continued to hold up her mother end of the bargain.

But as a son he'd dropped the ball a long time ago. And now it was time he picked the blasted thing back up.

He grudgingly admitted that a lot had changed in his view of the world since he'd met Laney. For a man as set in his ways as he'd believed himself to be, she'd easily taken his stubborn chin in her soft, white hands and turned his head from here to there, showing him different landscapes, making him see beyond his narrow view.

And there wasn't a day, an hour, a minute, a second that went by that he didn't remember what it was like to have her in his life. Not a moment passed when he didn't ache for her in a way that was shocking in its intensity.

He thought of calling her up. Showing up on her doorstep—which wouldn't be too difficult because every now and again he found his bike leading him to her apartment building, where he'd sit for a time watching for her, even if she no longer needed looking after.

"One of man's greatest flaws is thinking he can conquer a problem by hitting it with the same ole hammer."

Carter rubbed his chin, remembering group leader Gary Nussom's words yesterday at the biweekly meetings he'd begun attending. Like him, Gary was a Marine, now retired. But no matter the twenty years Nussom had on him, he openly admitted to nightmares and nightly sweats and waking up filled with a bloodlust that left him shaking.

Who needed drugs, he'd asked, when war could screw up your mind far more than a drink, a puff, a snort or a needle? And the damage was permanent. You could use some tools to help deal with it, but it would always be there. To the very day you died.

Carter never thought himself the kind of guy to get into this sort of shit. And he certainly hadn't participated to the extent that Nussom would have liked for the first couple of weeks. But gradually he was coming to understand that he wasn't alone. And they weren't alone. And by accepting that, he was beginning to open up in a way that he never could as a true blood, Devil Dog Marine.

While in the beginning he might have convinced himself that he was just going through the motions, attending the meetings so he might earn his way back into the Corps, it didn't take him long to understand that he didn't want to go back. Maybe at some point in the future, but not now.

The Corps had been right in suspending him. He'd been in no mental shape to be out there on the front lines where he imagined enemies everywhere. And he had no idea when that might change.

So he'd gone ahead and used the money he'd saved up while stationed away from home and bought Old Man Johnson's closed-up auto repair shop. No sooner had he pried the boards off the windows than he began getting business from Johnson's old customers, some looking for an oil change, others a tire rotation. Most of the vehicles needed repairs that might have been ignored a year ago, with the owners trading them in for new models. But in the current economic mess, repairs seemed to be the name of the game.

Business already, and he hadn't officially opened his doors yet. Three weeks in, and he was interviewing mechanics. One of the neighborhood teenagers hanging around the place was helping out without pay—something Carter was going to change when he got back with a nice, fat check. Some customers made cracks about Naomi being a girl, but Ni had proven herself gifted when it came to a car engine, and Carter had no intention of letting her go anywhere.

Still, no matter what he did to occupy his time—be it fixing up the shop and repairing cars, renovating his father's old shack of a house or attending group meetings—he couldn't seem to escape one small fact: he missed Laney like hell.

What was the saying? Time heals all wounds? He snorted. Right.

Then there was another one. Absence makes the heart grow fonder. Now *that* he could relate to. Only fondness didn't come close to describing his almost crippling need for her.

So you've been punishing every woman who's crossed your path for your mother's sins.

Laney's words, spoken while she was spooned against his body in all her nude glory, had haunted him ever since she'd said them.

Could she be right? Was that why he never let a woman closer than arm's length? Oh, he could have sex with them. But anything beyond that was forbidden territory. Even with her.

Especially with her.

He punched at the truck's radio station buttons, searching out a song that didn't have to do with crying into somebody else's beer, tractors or unfaithful ex-lovers, and then shut off the radio altogether, earning him a look from Blue.

"What?" he asked the old hound. "Did I interrupt your slobber session?"

Blue licked his chops and went back to pole watching.

The whole class thing, he knew it was all just so much superficial bullshit. While he admitted discomfort at the wealth her father displayed, the problem lay not with her father, but with himself.

And that was the real reason he was heading down to see his mother, wasn't it? To figure out how much his own father had screwed his head up. And get his mother's perspective so he could help screw it back the other way so it would finally be straight.

His expectations were high. But he had to try. Because one thing he knew beyond a shadow of a doubt was that he was going to do all he could to get Laney back. He'd just prefer to do it as a better man. And he wasn't talking about money, either.

Although it had been years since he'd visited, Carter knew the way to his mother's house as if he'd been driving there all his life. In a way, he had. Emotionally. Her whereabouts had been one constant in his ever-changing world. And while he had never turned to her, somehow he had always known he could.

He pulled up in the driveway of the medium-sized house in an older Austin subdivision, noting the green lawn and the colorful flowers and the Welcome sign on a homemade wreath on the door. He'd called her yesterday to tell her he was coming. She hadn't hesitated when she told him she'd be waiting.

He shut off the truck engine, listening to the sounds around him—children playing basketball, a lawn mower, birds. Then he slowly got out, holding the door open for Blue to jump down. He was halfway up the walk when the front door opened and there stood his mother, smiling at him as if he'd just seen her yesterday…as if she'd been waiting for this moment for a long, long time and now it was finally here.

HAD FOUR WEEKS PASSED since she'd last seen Carter? Laney wondered with no small amount of surprise as she stood in front of her office window looking out. Gone were the neat downtown streets, replaced by those of the more sparsely populated, industrial south side of town. She smiled. While the new view didn't have quite the cachet of her former office, neither did it have the isolation or the pressures from her superiors.

As she'd suspected, senior partner Harold Reasoner had a large bone to pick with her over how she'd handled the MacGregor case. She'd been prepared, so that the instant he made a veiled threat to terminate her association with the firm, she'd quit on the spot.

It had taken her a week to pass on her active case files, clear the clients who wanted to follow her to her new solo practice and make the needed arrangements for her new business address.

Of course, having Violet along for the ride helped immensely.

"There is no way you're leaving me here all alone," she'd told Laney matter-of-factly when Laney shared the news of her departure.

The office of Laney Cartwright, Attorney-at-Law, consisted of three rooms. A small lobby, Violet's office and then her own. It was nowhere near as posh as her former surroundings, but that's just how she wanted it. She had no intention of catering strictly to those who could afford her previous firm's exorbitant fees. While she wouldn't turn them away, either, she wanted to open her doors to a wider variety of clients, many of which would be sent her way via the Dallas Public Defenders Office, with whom she'd contracted to handle a minimum number of criminal cases.

She didn't fool herself into thinking that clients from a lower-income group would be any more honest than Devon MacGregor had been. But she'd handle that aspect when the time came, with no one above her telling her which cases she had to take or pass on.

And the first client she'd signed up was Tiffany Mullins.

"Where do you want this?" Violet asked, struggling with a plant nearly as tall as she was.

"Not another one." Laney hurried across the room to help her put it down near the dozen other plants and floral arrangements she'd been receiving steadily since announcing the opening of her new office. She looked for a card. "Who's this one from?"

"You're not going to believe it, but I think Reasoner sent it." Violet frowned in obvious distaste. "Probably had his secretary pick it out."

Laney read the congratulatory wishes and then put the card on her desk along with the others. "Huh."

Violet leaned against the doorjamb. "Never hurts to keep the lines of communication open. Especially since you're going to be sitting in as consultant on a couple of the cases you left behind."

"Right," Laney said, wondering at how incestuous the legal profession was.

Of course, she'd already seen many of her former coworkers at a recent symphony charity event, so she needed no reminders of how tight the Dallas business community was. Still, there were some people she didn't care if she ever saw again. And that thought would never have crossed her mind before…

Before Carter.

Violet went back to her own office, leaving Laney alone with her thoughts. Which was never a good idea. Because the more time she had to think, the more her thoughts turned to Carter.

Okay, so maybe her heart did lurch in hope every time a delivery came. Was it too much to hope that he might send her something?

Then again, for all she knew, he was back in the Marines and stationed halfway across the world.

She refused to allow herself to call his JAG attorney to check up on him. But with every day that passed, her resolve eroded just a little bit more.

"So call him."

Not her words, but her father's—at lunch earlier that day.

"What?" she'd said, sitting across from him at Raphael's and forking poached salmon she had no intention of eating.

"I said call him." Her father's eyes had a knowing glint in them as he'd sipped his water. "You've been awful company all month. Ever since you stopped seeing the Marine."

"Carter," she corrected.

"So call him."

Could it really be that simple?

Could she just pick up the phone and rid her heart of the ache that threatened to swallow it and her whole?

"Look, Laney," her father had said, "I'm just going to say this once, and then we never have to talk about it again if you don't want to. But it's obvious you love the guy."

Her eyes had burned with unshed tears, rendering her speechless.

"Have you told him how you feel?"

Of course, she hadn't. It had all happened too soon to sort everything out. Too fast for her to get her feet under her. To figure out what she wanted.

And then the decision had been taken out of her hands and she'd let it go.

"That doesn't mean you can't grab it back," her father had said.

A slow smile spread across Laney's face.

Grab it back, indeed.

She reached for the phone, dialing a number she knew by heart, and suspected she always would.

22

ON THE DRIVE back to Dallas three days later, Carter felt as if someone had taken him by the shoulders, dunked him in a giant tub of soapy water and then hauled him out to dry in the fresh Texas sunshine. Group therapy was partially to credit for his new take on life. His three-day visit with his mother and extended family was also responsible. Both had laid the foundation for his response to Laney's phone call.

His cell phone had rung the first day of his Austin visit as he'd stood at the kitchen door of his mother's house, watching her spray his niece and two nephews with a hose in a plastic pool. They'd even splashed Blue, who had run around like a puppy rather than the old hound he was. It had been an hour before dinner, and she had invited him to stay. An hour before, he had been welcomed by his half brothers and half sister with open arms as if he'd been away on assignment rather than by choice. His mother and he had had a four-hour conversation about all they had missed, and all they intended to make up for.

Seeing Laney's name on his cell phone display had made his throat feel tight. He'd answered on the third ring.

"Carter?"

The knots in his stomach had unfurled as if coaxed open by her sweet voice. "Hello, Laney."

He'd heard the clutch of her throat, her nervousness reflecting his. "I was wondering how you were doing."

He'd watched as his mother dried her hands on a towel and headed back in his direction. "I'm fine. And you?"

"Fine. Fine."

A long pause made him want to be next to her instead of halfway across the state. "Look, Laney, I'm out of town now—"

"Are you back in the Corps?" she asked with obvious alarm.

"No, no. Just down in Austin for a few days. Can I call you when I get back?"

He could almost see her smiling. "Yes. I'd like that."

He'd hung up immediately, but not before his mother caught him on the phone.

He was coming to learn that there was such a thing as mother's radar. Mary Manson had the ability to pluck items from his brain the moment he thought them.

It wasn't that his father had been any less observant. He guessed there were just some things men weren't as well equipped to deal with as women. Or maybe women were just more willing to give them a try.

His mother had instantly homed in on the fact he'd been talking to a woman. Not any woman, but one that meant a great deal to him.

So as he helped her prepare a dinner that would

include the entire family, keeping an eye on the playing children in the back, he'd told her about him and Laney. He'd weathered looks of pain and encouragement, and then when he was done, she'd taken the basket of bread he'd sliced from his hands and urged him to face her. He'd stared down into a face that looked so much like his own it almost hurt to think how long he'd gone without enjoying it.

"Don't close yourself off to Laney, Carter. Don't ever let something small like class prevent you from loving the person you want. Your dad did that with me."

He'd glimpsed the pain there, the pain she must have felt so many years before when his father had pushed her out of their lives.

"I never stopped loving your father, Carter. Love, true love, is something that never fades, never goes away." He'd wanted to hand her a tissue or a paper towel to wipe the tears about to spill from her bright eyes. But she refused to release him from her gaze. "Make the decisions you have to, but remember that the way you feel now, you will feel always. It's what you do with those feelings that can mean the difference between happiness and a lifetime of pain."

"But you went on to create another life," he'd said quietly.

"Yes, yes, I did. But only when I knew there was no hope left in returning to the one I'd made with your father. With you." She'd looked down and then quickly back up, as if afraid to break the connection. "I've gone on to love again. And am happier than any one woman has a right to be. But that first love…it's always there. And it was only with your father's passing that I was truly set free to love fully again."

She touched the side of his face and smiled.

"You're so much like your father, Carter."

He'd grimaced.

"No, no. It's a good thing. A very good thing. You're strong and loyal and have this incredible capacity for love." She'd swallowed hard. "Don't let fear rob you of happiness. Like fear robbed your father and me of ours."

Fear. Was that ultimately what was holding him back from giving his all to Laney? Fear of what would happen if he completely surrendered to his feelings for her? Fear of getting hurt? Of being rejected? Rejected by her and the society she belonged to?

Of one day waking up and finding the passion gone and Laney gone with it?

He was on the outskirts of Dallas now. Despite it being dinnertime on Sunday, the traffic was heavy and he turned up the radio to drown out the sound of a pair of motorcycles passing to his left. He gave a little salute to the two riders and then listened as Blue threw his head back in the passenger's seat and issued a low and long howl, singing along with Clint Black.

"I hear you, brother," he said to the old hound, patting him heartily on the back. "I hear you."

He had yet to call Laney back. Was even beginning to wonder if it was the right thing to do, despite his visit with his mother. He had so much to work out, to absorb. Maybe he'd wait a little while before inviting her into the chaos.

The thought incited a sharp pain to rip across his chest. He ignored it as he exited the highway and set his direction for the final stretch toward home.

The instant he pulled up into the gravel driveway of his small house, he knew something was off. The front door was open and music drifted out, country and western. He shut off the truck engine and opened the door, taken aback when Blue rushed over him and jumped out first, running to the front steps in a way he hadn't done before.

One of his neighbors? It seemed the most likely guess. Julia Jackson had cleaned up a bit once or twice before when he was stationed in the Middle East and due for leave. Then there was Naomi, who was a resourceful kid and had some trouble at home with a drunken stepfather. Could she have needed a place to stay and crashed here?

Either way, it wouldn't be difficult to gain access. Since he didn't own much worth taking, he often didn't lock the back door, figuring a broken window would be more costly to replace than anything a burglar might take.

He climbed out of the truck and walked up to the steps, opening the screen door to let Blue in before entering himself. Someone was singing softly. A female somebody.

Carter tossed his overnight bag to the living room floor and walked toward the kitchen, where the sounds were coming from. He stopped there in the doorway, his breath stolen straight from his body.

There at the ancient stove stood none other than an angel in blue.

Laney.

A million thoughts rushed through his mind as he took in the back of the simple linen tank dress she wore, her feet bare against tile that had been mopped, her short blond hair curling every which way as she hummed the parts of the Carrie Underwood song she didn't know the words to that played on the transistor radio in the window.

He'd never brought her here, but he figured it wouldn't have been difficult for her to find out where he lived. It was probably listed on the papers his JAG attorney had forwarded to her.

What she was doing there was another matter entirely.

Blue half galloped, half lumbered his way to press his wet nose against the back of her knee. Carter watched as she gasped and then crouched down to pat the old hound, who was as happy to see her as Carter was.

"Hey, Blue. How are you doing, boy?"

Carter felt as if his heart had grown to the size of a summer watermelon even as he noted that the hound was no kind of watchdog.

Seeming to realize that if Blue was there, then his owner had likely also returned, Laney slowly stood up and turned to face Carter.

The watermelon pitched to Carter's booted feet. Christ, she was even more beautiful than he remembered. But it was more than the sum of her physical characteristics. It was in the way she looked at him, as if the sun rose and set on him.

Her elegant throat worked around a swallow. "Um, I hope you don't mind. I just thought I'd come over and make dinner for you." She gestured toward the stove. "You've fed me so often that I figured it was time I returned the favor."

Was she afraid that he'd be angry with her? He suspected she was. But damned if he could do anything about it. His boots seemed cemented to the floor.

"How did you know I would be coming back tonight?" he asked.

She smiled and tucked an errant curl behind a perfectly formed shell of an ear. "I didn't. That's why there's already two days' worth of dinners in the refrigerator."

She seemed uneasy with the confession and bit her plump bottom lip.

That this self-assured, confident woman could be so nervous touched Carter beyond words. But even as the observation crossed his mind, he watched as Laney reacted to his lack of response. Her round shoulders pulled back slightly and her chin went up just a bit.

"Are you telling me I'm not welcome?"

Carter grinned and shook his head. Oh, she was more than welcome. She was the answer to all of his prayers.

Before he was consciously aware of wanting to make the move, he'd crossed the room and hauled Laney into his arms, holding her as close as he dared, pressing his hands over her soft back, into her silken curls. And when he kissed her, he did so with an honesty that not even he could mask.

Her low moan spoke volumes as she returned his needy attention, curving her leg around his knee and rubbing her calf against his restlessly even as she thrust her fingers into the back of his hair.

"God, this past month has been hell without you," she whispered against his mouth as he kissed her again. "I feel as if I've spent my entire life trying to live up to a list of expectations. Expectations from my father, from my friends, from myself..." She kissed him long and hard. "And then you came into my life and I felt that bridle of expectations cut into my soul."

He couldn't seem to get enough of her, and predicted that he never would.

"I love you, Carter. I'm not afraid to say that anymore. I love you."

He kissed her more deeply, drinking in her sweet essence and the warm shadow in her eyes.

"Laney, sweet Laney. I love you so damn much it hurts to breathe."

He stared at her, his heart pounding in his chest.

Then she smiled and pressed her nose against his. "So now what do we do?"

"We ride this road and see where it takes us."

If he'd once feared that road might dead-end or run out, he wasn't anymore. So long as he had her along for the ride, he suspected they could circle the globe twice and still find something new and exciting to see.

A burning smell eclipsed the scent of her hair even as Blue let rip a howling bark.

"But first," he suggested, "it would be a good idea if we didn't let the place burn down around our ears."

"The garlic bread!" Laney stepped out of his embrace and then turned around to open the oven door. She attempted to take the bread out with her hands and then grabbed a towel instead, tossing the half-blackened loaf to the counter.

Carter took in the bubbling tomato sauce in one pan and the boiling pasta in another on the stovetop. She was making him spaghetti.

He spotted a pie in the window next to the radio. She turned off the stovetop burners and followed his gaze.

"Blueberry pie. I'd like to take credit, but the truth is a couple of your neighbors brought it over an hour or so ago."

"Did they, now?" Word that Carter had a woman at his place would have made the grapevine by now and he'd be hit with even more offerings, his other neighbors looking for a juicy tidbit or two about Laney and him.

"You've been staying here?" he asked.

Laney's chin came up again. "Yes, I have. I waited until late the first night and, well, decided I should just sleep over rather than drive back into town."

Carter couldn't believe Laney had stayed the night in his place, or that she looked at home doing it.

All his fears of how she might judge him if she saw

his place exited on an exhale. He'd been stupid to think she'd be so shallow.

"I know you were reluctant about bringing me here," she said quietly, seeming to read his mind in that way he was coming to think any woman close to him could. "And I won't pretend to understand why, beyond your house being modest. But the truth is, I've enjoyed being surrounded by your things."

"My things, huh?" he asked, advancing on her.

Laney leaned her back against the sink. "Uh-huh."

"And just how many of my things are you talking about?"

Her smile aimed sunshine into every shadowy corner of his soul. "Oh, everything."

He cocked a brow. "Everything?"

"Mmm."

He laced her arms over his shoulders and then lifted her so that her legs hugged his hips, her feet crossing behind his back.

"Well, okay," she said, restlessly licking her lips as she stared hungrily at his mouth. "Maybe not everything."

He kissed her and turned to walk toward his closed bedroom door.

"But there is one thing I did change. I hope you don't mind."

Carter barely heard her as he turned the knob and kicked the door open.

There in the middle of his bedroom sat a king-size bed covered with a multicolored quilt and dozens of pillows.

He looked at her.

She shrugged. "That twin bed just wasn't going to do."

"No," he admitted, wondering what other kinds of changes were in store for him. And for the first time looking forward to every last one of them.

Blue's nails clicked against the floor as he followed them. Carter blocked him with his boot and then nudged him back out.

"Your food's in the other room, boy," he said and closed the door. He gazed down at the woman in his arms. "This meal's all mine."

* * * * *

*Celebrate Harlequin's 60th anniversary with
Harlequin® Superromance®
and the DIAMOND LEGACY miniseries!*

*Follow the stories of four cousins as they come to
terms with the complications of love and what it means
to be a family. Discover with them the sixty-year-old
secret that rocks not one but two families in…
A DAUGHTER'S TRUST by Tara Taylor Quinn.*

*Available in September 2009 from
Harlequin® Superromance®*

RICK'S APPOINTMENT with his attorney early Wednesday morning went only moderately better than his meeting with social services the day before. The prognosis wasn't great—but at least his attorney was going to file a motion for DNA testing. Just so Rick could petition to see the child…his sister's baby. The sister he didn't know he had until it was too late.

The rest of what his attorney said had been downhill from there.

Cell phone in hand before he'd even reached his Nitro, Rick punched in the speed dial number he'd programmed the day before.

Maybe foster parent Sue Bookman hadn't received his message. Or had lost his number. Maybe she didn't want to talk to him. At this point he didn't much care what she wanted.

"Hello?" She answered before the first ring was complete. And sounded breathless.

Young and breathless.

"Ms. Bookman?"

"Yes. This is Rick Kraynick, right?"

"Yes, ma'am."

"I recognized your number on caller ID," she said,

her voice uneven, as though she was still engaged in whatever physical activity had her so breathless to begin with. "I'm sorry I didn't get back to you. I've been a little…distracted."

The words came in more disjointed spurts. Was she jogging?

"No problem," he said, when, in fact, he'd spent the better part of the night before watching his phone. And fretting. "Did I get you at a bad time?"

"No worse than usual," she said, adding, "Better than some. So, how can I help?"

God, if only this could be so easy. He'd ask. She'd help. And life could go well. At least for one little person in his family.

It would be a first.

"Mr. Kraynick?"

"Yes. Sorry. I was… Are you sure there isn't a better time to call?"

"I'm bouncing a baby, Mr. Kraynick. It's what I do."

"Is it Carrie?" he asked quickly, his pulse racing.

"How do you know Carrie?" She sounded defensive, which wouldn't do him any good.

"I'm her uncle," he explained, "her mother's— Christy's—older brother, and I know you have her."

"I can neither confirm nor deny your allegations, Mr. Kraynick. Please call social services." She rattled off the number.

"Wait!" he said, unable to hide his urgency. "Please," he said more calmly. "Just hear me out."

"How did you find me?"

"A friend of Christy's."

"I'm sorry I can't help you, Mr. Kraynick," she said softly. "This conversation is over."

"I grew up in foster care," he said, as though that gave him some special privilege. Some insider's edge.

"Then you know you shouldn't be calling me at all."

"Yes… But Carrie is my niece," he said. "I need to see her. To know that she's okay."

"You'll have to go through social services to arrange that."

"I'm sure you know it's not as easy as it sounds. I'm a single man with no real ties and I've no intention of petitioning for custody. They aren't real eager to give me the time of day. I never even knew Carrie's mother. For all intents and purposes, our mother didn't raise either one of us. All I have going for me is half a set of genes. My lawyer's on it, but it could be weeks—months—before this is sorted out. Carrie could be adopted by then. Which would be fine, great for her, but then I'd have lost my chance. I don't want to take her. I won't hurt her. I just have to see her."

"I'm sorry, Mr. Kraynick, but…"

* * * * *

*Find out if Rick Kraynick will ever have a chance
to meet his niece.
Look for A DAUGHTER'S TRUST
by Tara Taylor Quinn,
available September 2009.*

We'll be spotlighting a different series
every month throughout 2009
to celebrate our 60th anniversary.

Look for Harlequin® Superromance®
in September!

*Celebrate with
The Diamond Legacy
miniseries!*

Follow the stories of four cousins as they come to terms
with the complications of love and what it means to
be a family. Discover with them the sixty-year-old secret
that rocks not one but two families.

A DAUGHTER'S TRUST by *Tara Taylor Quinn*
September

FOR THE LOVE OF FAMILY by *Kathleen O'Brien*
October

LIKE FATHER, LIKE SON by *Karina Bliss*
November

A MOTHER'S SECRET by *Janice Kay Johnson*
December

Available wherever books are sold.

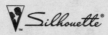

SPECIAL EDITION

FROM *NEW YORK TIMES* BESTSELLING AUTHOR

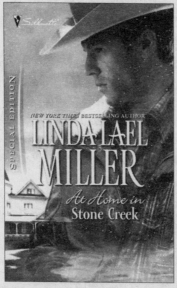

Ashley O'Ballivan had her heart broken by a man years ago—and now he's mysteriously back. Jack McCall *isn't* the person she thinks he is. For her sake, he must keep his distance, but his feelings for her are powerful. To protect her—from his enemies and himself—he has to leave...vowing to fight his way home to her and Stone Creek forever.

Available in November wherever books are sold.

Visit Silhouette Books at www.eHarlequin.com

You're invited to join our Tell Harlequin Reader Panel!

By joining our new reader panel you will:

- Receive Harlequin® books—they are FREE and yours to keep with no obligation to purchase anything!
- Participate in fun online surveys
- Exchange opinions and ideas with women just like you
- Have a say in our new book ideas and help us publish the best in women's fiction

In addition, you will have a chance to win great prizes and receive special gifts!
See Web site for details. Some conditions apply.
Space is limited.

To join, visit us at
www. TellHarlequin.com.

REQUEST YOUR FREE BOOKS!

2 FREE NOVELS PLUS 2 FREE GIFTS!

HARLEQUIN®

Blaze™

Red-hot reads!

YES! Please send me 2 FREE Harlequin® Blaze™ novels and my 2 FREE gifts (gifts are worth about $10). After receiving them, if I don't wish to receive any more books, I can return the shipping statement marked "cancel". If I don't cancel, I will receive 6 brand-new novels every month and be billed just $4.24 per book in the U.S. or $4.71 per book in Canada. That's a savings of 15% off the cover price. It's quite a bargain. Shipping and handling is just 50¢ per book.* I understand that accepting the 2 free books and gifts places me under no obligation to buy anything. I can always return a shipment and cancel at any time. Even if I never buy another book, the two free books and gifts are mine to keep forever.

151 HDN EYS2 351 HDN EYTE

Name	(PLEASE PRINT)	
Address		Apt. #
City	State/Prov.	Zip/Postal Code

Signature (if under 18, a parent or guardian must sign)

Mail to the **Harlequin Reader Service:**
IN U.S.A.: P.O. Box 1867, Buffalo, NY 14240-1867
IN CANADA: P.O. Box 609, Fort Erie, Ontario L2A 5X3

Not valid to current subscribers of Harlequin Blaze books.

Want to try two free books from another line?
Call 1-800-873-8635 or visit www.morefreebooks.com.

* Terms and prices subject to change without notice. Prices do not include applicable taxes. N.Y. residents add applicable sales tax. Canadian residents will be charged applicable provincial taxes and GST. Offer not valid in Quebec. This offer is limited to one order per household. All orders subject to approval. Credit or debit balances in a customer's account(s) may be offset by any other outstanding balance owed by or to the customer. Please allow 4 to 6 weeks for delivery. Offer available while quantities last.

Your Privacy: Harlequin Books is committed to protecting your privacy. Our Privacy Policy is available online at www.eHarlequin.com or upon request from the Reader Service. From time to time we make our lists of customers available to reputable third parties who may have a product or service of interest to you. If you would prefer we not share your name and address, please check here. ☐

HB09R

Stay up-to-date on all your romance reading news!

The Harlequin Inside Romance newsletter is a **FREE** quarterly newsletter highlighting our upcoming series releases and promotions!

Go to eHarlequin.com/InsideRomance

or e-mail us at
InsideRomance@Harlequin.com
to sign up to receive
your **FREE** newsletter today!

HARLEQUIN *Blaze*™

COMING NEXT MONTH

Available August 25, 2009

#489 GETTING PHYSICAL Jade Lee

For American student/waitress Zoe Lewis, Tantric sex—sex as a spiritual experience—is a totally foreign concept. Strange, yet irresistible. Then she's partnered with Tantric master Stephen Chiu…and discovers just how far great sex can take a girl!

#490 MADE YOU LOOK Jamie Sobrato
Forbidden Fantasies

She spies with her little eye… From the privacy of her living room Arianna Day has a front-row seat for her neighbor Noah Quinn's sex forays. And she knows he's the perfect man to end her bout of celibacy. Now to come up with the right plan to make him look…

#491 TEXAS HEAT Debbi Rawlins
Encounters

Four college girlfriends arrive at the Sugarloaf ranch to celebrate an engagement announcement. With all the tasty cowboys around, each will have a reunion weekend she'll never forget!

#492 FEELS LIKE THE FIRST TIME Tawny Weber
Dressed to Thrill

Zoe Gaston hated high school. So the thought of going back for her reunion doesn't exactly thrill her. Little does she guess that there's a really hot guy who's been waiting ten long years to do just that!

#493 HER LAST LINE OF DEFENSE Marie Donovan
Uniformly Hot!

Instructing a debutante in survival training is not how Green Beret Luc Boudreau planned to spend his temporary leave. Problem is, he kind of likes this feisty fish out of water and it turns out the feeling's mutual. But will they find any common ground other than their shared bedroll…?

#494 ONE GOOD MAN Alison Kent
American Heroes: The Texas Rangers

Jamie Danby needs a hero—badly. As the only witness to a brutal shooting, she's been flying below the radar for years. Now her cover's blown and she needs a sexy Texas Ranger around 24/7 to make her feel safe. The best sex of her life is just a bonus!

HBCNMBPA0809